'Waste him!' yelped a voice from the blackness, and Herne dived to his left, snapping off a couple of shots into the alley.

A volley of shooting came whining back at him, the bullets digging sand up all around him. But the light was poor and he was a moving target.

'Jesus!' Herne screamed, rolling over and over, holding his stomach as though he'd been gut-hit, making sure that he ended up in the cover of a horse-trough, in case they had a long gun with them and just pumped a few slugs into him to make sure that he wasn't faking . . .

Also in this series:

HERNE THE HUNTER 1: WHITE DEATH
HERNE THE HUNTER 2: RIVER OF BLOOD
HERNE THE HUNTER 3: THE BLACK WIDOW
HERNE THE HUNTER 4: SHADOW OF THE VULTURE
HERNE THE HUNTER 5: APACHE SQUAW
HERNE THE HUNTER 6: DEATH IN GOLD

and published by Corgi Books

John J. McLaglen

Herne The Hunter 7: Death Rites

CORGI BOOKS
A DIVISION OF TRANSWORLD PUBLISHERS LTD

HERNE THE HUNTER 7: DEATH RITES

A CORGI BOOK 0 552 10720 4

First publication in Great Britain

PRINTING HISTORY
Corgi edition published 1978

Corgi Books are published by
Transworld Publishers Ltd
Century House, 61–63 Uxbridge Road,
Ealing, London W5 5SA

Made and printed in Great Britain by
Cox & Wyman Ltd, London, Reading and Fakenham

This is for Mike Tarrant and Don Day who make such a great job of riding shotgun on the Mother Lode. With sincere thanks.

Chapter One

The sails of the ship fluttered like so many giant birds as they were reefed ready for coming into harbour.

Jed Herne hunched his shoulders against the cold and pulled the hat down over his face. He leaned back against the wall at the end of the dock, keeping well clear of the other people who also waited for their relatives and friends newly returned from Europe.

Soon the ship was close enough for him to pick out the name written about the prow, to see the slight figure of a girl straining over the deck rail as though she could scarcely wait for the ship to dock.

Herne glanced upwards as thick flakes of snow began suddenly to tumble down from out of the grey sky. He looked at the pale, searching face of the girl.

Winter had come.

And so had Becky.

'Cold as damned charity!'

'Colder'n a grizzly's asshole!'

The third man in the group added nothing to the conversation. Unsurprisingly, because he was a mute, his tongue having been ripped from his mouth in a bitter waterfront brawl some eight years back.

They stood a few paces behind Jedediah Herne, watching the docking of the big sailing-ship. Occasionally one of them would gob into the iron-grey waters of the Hudson River or point at one of the little oyster boats that darted in between the berthing vessel and the wharves. An unsavoury trio and obviously up to no good.

Herne had noticed them, as he noticed everything that went on around him. In a couple of months he would be celebrating his fortieth birthday. Most of his life he had spent with a gun on his hip, and the knowledge that he had the ability to use it fast and deadly. You didn't even live to be twenty if you didn't learn early to watch everything going on.

Few gunmen lived to be thirty.

Jed didn't know anyone else who'd got as close to forty as he had.

Then again, Jed Herne – Herne the Hunter – was someone very special.

The girl on the deck waved down to him, and he waved back, the movement lifting the tails of his coat, revealing the heavy leather belt.

'Money-belt,' hissed one of the trio of wharf rats, pointing to it. His two comrades nodded their agreement, and looked more carefully at the man in front of them.

Greying hair, under the hat. Westerner, they guessed, grinning inwardly as they thought how easy it was going to be to take the rube for what he'd got. Tall and broad. Couple of inches over six feet, and something around the two hundred pound mark.

That was what they saw.

They didn't see the Colt with the polished grips, settling snug in the greased holster, tied to the top of the right thigh. Nor did they see the honed bayonet, a memento of the Civil War.

'Take him after she's docked. On the way out. Looks like all he's waitin' for's that little girl with the white face up yonder.'

It was going to be so easy.

There were three of them to one of him.

All of them had knives, and wicked little leather pouches filled with lead shot that could sink into a man's skull as gentle as winking.

They relaxed, drawing up the collars of their jackets against the pattering bolts of hail which were hissing off the Hudson, and waited.

Having noted their presence, Jed chose to ignore them and concentrated once more on the girl. On Becky.

It was nearly two years since the night that had changed his life and left him with sole responsibility for the young girl. She'd been fourteen then. A solitary child with a stubborn jaw and deep-set, serious eyes. Living with her parents, Rachel and Bill Yates, on the spread right next to the one outside Tucson where Jed lived with his young wife, Louise.

Friday, March 20th, 1879.

That had been the date. After that night Jed had lost his wife, and Rebecca Yates had lost her mother. With the passing of Louise, Jed also lost the only person who had been able to check his killing progress. A progress that he had known would finally end with a bullet in the back and a dusty plot on Boot Hill. Marrying Louise had changed all that. The Colt had been wrapped in an oiled cloth and stached away in a drawer. The fifty-five Sharps rifle had been hung on the wall.

Then it was over.

Disappeared in a welter of blood and screaming violence. The killings had only begun with Louise and Rachel Yates. Soon after that, Becky's father had ridden that one-way path.

After the men who had wrecked his life were all cleansed from the earth, Jed started looking around him.

Seeing the young girl who depended on him for her education. For everything. He had sent her to Europe to be educated away from the slaughter that followed him across America. Financing her fancy schooling by killing men. Too many men.*

Now she was coming home again, presenting him with a whole set of problems. Where to live? How to live?

And there was another problem. One that Jed Herne only ever set his mind to in the waking hours of the early morning, when the body sweats and thoughts rove freely. Becky was now sixteen. Just the age that Louise had been when she had married the infamous Herne the Hunter. And Becky was just as pretty . . .

Life was going to be hard.

Damned hard.

It took a little over an hour to get the girl through the formalities. There was the usual delay over documentation, and the light was beginning to fade across the murky expanse of the Hudson when Jed Herne finally saw the slight figure coming off the ship, resting her hand on the rail of the gangplank. Halfway down she stopped, and he thought that she was going to fall, but she paused and recovered. He guessed that she must be suffering from the rigours of the long sea crossing.

Becky had never been the strongest of girls, liable to catch a cold on the least excuse. He well remembered the winter evenings on their homestead near Tucson when Becky would come and sit with Louise, their heads close together while they giggled over some joke. He would be resting, with maybe a book open on his lap. Another habit that he had

* *The details of the previous two years in the life of Jedediah Herne can be read in the six earlier titles in the series, all from Corgi Books.*

caught from his young wife. There had been the bursts of coughing that had sometimes been severe enough to make Becky weep, her eyes starting from her head with the strain, while Louise had taken her hand to try and comfort her.

But the weather in Europe must have been kinder than the winters in Arizona.

'Jed!'

'Becky!'

There was fog rolling in off the East River shore, slowly, slowly covering the city. Masking the filth that lay all about their feet on the dock, softening the harsh lines of the wet warehouse roofs. Dulling the stench of the Hudson that rolled by a few yards from where they met.

Her face was hidden in a poke bonnet of dark blue, and Jed wasn't able to see her. But she had grown taller, and there was more than the suggestion of a womanish figure blooming where there had once been only the gawky bones of a coltish girl.

'Oh, Jed, I'm so . . .' and she started to cough, so that he reached out for her, wanting to swing her up in his arms and hold her to him, but knowing that she was too tall and grown for that.

He clasped her, and was hard put to suppress a gasp of shock and dismay at her lightness. It was like holding a frail little bird to him, and he could feel her heart pounding through the thick layers of cloak that enveloped her.

'Becky!'

'I'll . . . Oh, my goodness . . . It's this goshdarned fog that bites so . . .'

He held her to him, not wanting to squeeze her too hard in case he crushed her brittle ribs that he could feel against his chest. Waiting for the paroxysm to pass so that he could lead her from the deserted wharf and into a cab and to the warmth of the hotel.

Few folks made the trip across the Atlantic at that time of year unless they had to, and already the officials had made their way off. Leaving the dock to Jed and Becky. And behind them, dim shadows against the grey darkness, skulked the three wharf rats.

Waiting.

'Becky. I'm real pleased to see you again. We got loads to talk about.'

Now that she was here, Jed felt strangely cold towards her. A distant formality seemed to have his body in its grip, so that he found himself making polite conversation, as if they had just been introduced at a Boston social.

Still she coughed, her chest heaving, clinging to him. In the evening cold he held her hand, unable to understand how her fingers could be so thin, like reeds, the nails rimmed with blue. She turned her face up to look at him, and he was unable to stop his jaw gaping at the sight.

The round face of the young girl was gone for ever. She had been pretty before. Now she was beautiful. But it was a strange, burning beauty. Her cheeks were pale, almost white, with two spots of hectic red heightening her cheek-bones. The eyes glowed with a desperate intensity, like pits of fire glimpsed at a great distance.

'I'm ill, Jed.'

'You'll get well again, Becky. It must have been the journey over. By God, but I recall being sick as a dyin' dog on a raft on the Colorado, never mind crossin' all that way across the sea.'

She shook her head, ringlets of dark hair blowing from under the fringe of her bonnet.

'No. I've had this cough ever since last Spring. Most times it's gone in the Summer, but it kind of lingered on. Now it's worse, and sometimes when I start to cough, it's like I can't stop.'

She was near tears, and Jedediah decided that she must be tired. The sooner they got out of the cold and damp of the wharf the better.

Slowly, with his arm close about her, Becky began to walk along the shadow of the line of towering buildings, aware of the slapping of the river at her side, the rough boards creaking beneath her feet.

'I'm so glad to be home again, Jed. It wasn't *that* awful, but I did miss you terribly. And this cough and cold seemed as if they would go on for ever.' She squeezed his arm in her hand. 'I feel so much better already, Jed. Much, much better.'

Despite the biting wind, Becky had pulled the front of her cloak open, and Jed saw the dying red light of the New York evening flashing on the pendant that Louise had given the girl. Only a small trinket, but it had been the property of his wife's grandparents. It was filigree silver, with a heart of tiny rubies set at its centre.

He was glad to see that she still wore it. Apart from a host of memories, that pendant was about the only thing he had with which to recall Louise. It wasn't a lot to bring back the three best years of his life.

'Come on. Not far to go. Sweet Jesus, Becky, but that wind is keener than a Comanche skinning knife.'

Together after the year apart, Jed Herne and Becky Yates walked in the solitary darkness towards the gates of the wharf. Their linked shadows followed them.

A few paces behind them, closing quickly, came three more shadows.

Very close.

Chapter Two

Jed's ears were filled with the harsh rasping of the girl's breath, so that he never heard the faint scrape of a boot on a fallen link of heavy chain.

It was Becky who heard it.

Half-turned.

Screamed.

Herne was hampered by the girl hanging on his arm. Desperately, he threw her away from him, seeing her sprawl out in a tangle of white legs, the scream dying away in a choking cough. One of the attackers kicked out at her as he closed in, and Jed heard the sickening thud of the foot making contact.

But there was no time to worry about Becky. He backed away from the assailants, fumbling under his coat for the Colt Peacemaker, unable to free the thong across the top of the hammer that held it secure.

A knife hissed through the air, plucking at the hem of his coat. Herne swung a left-hand punch to hold the man off.

There were three of them. Two tall and skinny, and the third hunched over and weaving in and out like a snake. All three wore a ragged collection of grey and black clothes, making it hard to pick them out against the bleak, rain-swept background.

All of them had knives, the points flickering in and out at

him. He stood back against a wall, balanced on the balls of his feet, trying to counter their moves.

'Come on, cowboy,' grinned one of his attackers, panting with the effort of keeping Herne pinned back.

'Yeah. Give up, country boy. Just stand still and let us take what we went. Maybe you won't get hurt too much.'

'And the little lady'll be safe as houses.'

'Sure. Bawdy houses!' yelped the other.

The third of them, bent to barely half the height of the others, barked his laughter, his voice gobbling in his throat like it was bubbling up through a cauldron of boiling phlegm.

Herne was like a dancer, trying to threaten the three dock-rats, even though he wasn't able to get at any of his weapons. The bayonet was snug in its holster in his right boot. To bend down for it would have been to invite a knife in the belly.

So it had to be the gun.

'You spoil our fun, rube, and we gonna cut you up real bad,' panted the leader of the attackers.

'Yeah. Cut us some of that tender meat I see lyin' still and waitin' for it, skirt up round her ass like she's waitin' just for us.'

'Peckerwood bastard!' snapped the first of them, beginning to lose patience.

Herne feinted an attack, forcing them all back a couple of steps, using the fraction of bought time to tear his coat open, the buttons popping across the wharf, flicking the retaining leather cord from the gun, feeling the cold of the walnut grips against his hand.

'Christ Almighty!' screeched one of the men as he saw the Colt spring into the cowboy's hand as if propelled there by a secret spring.

Jedediah Herne was faster than anything that they'd ever seen. Faster than anyone they were ever going to see.

The forty-five was in his hand, thumb pulling back the hammer with the triple click, revolving the chamber, so that the cartridge nestled ready.

As the fog closed in, the harbour was filling with the deep, mournful tones of sirens, all the ships giving warning of their positions. The noise drowned the first shot, the boom flat and muffled by the surrounding warehouses.

The bullet hit the leader of the three killers plumb in the centre of the chest, the impact of the heavy slug throwing him back on his heels. The knife tinkling on the wooden planks. Jed knew well the old gunfighter's saying: 'Never use one bullet when two'll do.'

He squeezed the thin trigger, filed down for speed of firing, seeing the flash of the muzzle bright in the failing light. Already rocked off balance, the impact of the second shot, high in the throat, toppled the attacker several steps backwards, his boots catching on the edge of the dock. He fell head over heels and landed with a faint splash in the freezing water.

Already dying, the would-be murderer wasn't able to kick his way to the surface. Before he could drown, the two bullets killed him, and he died feeling a bitter anger that he had failed against a western hick in a big hat.

By the time that his body hit the water, Jed had fired three more shots. Two of them smacking into the other tall man, doubling him up, sending him staggering from side to side, hands jammed against his stomach, trying to hold back the pain, moaning aloud. The third of the trio saw a half-chance and darted in, using his dying partner for cover. Jed snapped off a quick shot at him.

But he was unlucky. The bullet ripped into the top of the other man's head, exploding his skull into shards of splintered bone, pulverizing his brain into a ragged mess of pink and grey.

The mute hurdled the corpse, diving in at Herne, knife outstretched in his hand, a strangled yell bursting from his open mouth.

Two attackers down and dead with five bullets would have been good shooting at any time. But in the treacherous light, and the swirling mist, it was excellent. Yet with a third man leaping in at him, and one bullet left, Herne wished it could have been just that fraction better.

The acrid smell of the black powder smoke tugged at his nostrils as he dodged the attack, hearing the point of the knife grate on the wall immediately behind him. Reaching out with his left hand and tugging the smaller man by the collar, smothering his assault, making it hard for him to use the blade at such close quarters.

Pressing the muzzle of the pistol hard against the killer's stomach, feeling the roughness of the man's coat against the back of his knuckles.

Squeezing the trigger a sixth time.

The skinny body of the mute jerked as if it had been kicked by a swayback mule, and Herne waited for it to drop, pushing at it with the empty pistol. The man stepped back a couple of paces, the eyes blanking out with the beginning of the mystery of dying. The knife was still clutched firmly in his hand.

The mouth opened and closed a couple of times, but no sound came out. Herne risked a glance past the man to where Becky lay motionless, her hair spread out like a veil, the bonnet caught under her chin. It was too dark for Jed to see clearly, but there was a dark stain or a shadow about her open mouth.

It might have been a trick of the evening light.

It might have been blood.

Despite the severe gut-wound, the third man was coming back, knife ready, the other hand clutching the scorched mark on his coat where black blood was already trickling its way through the layers of winter clothing.

'Jesus,' said Herne quietly. 'I don't know what your name is, but you surely got a whole lot of nerve.'

He slipped the warm gun back into the holster, and dropped his hand to pull out the bayonet from inside the right boot.

It was a long weapon, slender and mean. Herne had carried that knife, or one like it, ever since his time in the War. As a boy of just nineteen he and his old friend Whitey Coburn had ridden with the notorious Quantrill. As part of his unit of Raiders they had been there on that bitter day in 1863 when the town of Lawrence had been burned to the ground and more than fifty men butchered. In that one year alone Quantrill and his men killed over a thousand people.

Neither Jed nor Whitey ever forgot those days.

Just as he looked after his guns, so Jedediah Herne never neglected his knife, keeping it honed sharp enough to split a hair.

A thread of scarlet worming from his open mouth, the mute lurched forwards, trying a clumsy stab at Herne, aiming at the groin. But Jed was faster and better balanced, with a longer knife. And he was without the handicap of a bullet in the stomach draining the life away.

He cut at the man's wrist, feeling the edge of his blade grate through flesh and tendon, opening up the fingers as if they'd been burned. His assailant's own knife slipped to the dock.

He tried to pick it up.

There wasn't any other kind of choice open to him.

And he didn't make it by a long way. As he stooped forwards, left hand still gripping the stomach wound, Herne stepped lightly in out of the fog at him, like the avenging angel of death, and cut his throat, the steel slicing a gaping mouth in the side of his neck, the blood from the severed artery under the ear spurting high in the air. Pattering on the damp wood all around them.

Gargling deep in his chest, the mute slipped to his knees like a penitent at confessional, one hand at his belly, the other touching the fountain of blood from his neck. He brought the dappled fingers to his eyes as if he couldn't believe what he was feeling.

Like a swimmer entering deep water, he slid forwards on his face, the blood slowing, dying away to a thin trickle, and finally stopping.

With the third death, Herne stood still, taking several deep breaths into his chest, relaxing himself after the supreme tension of the life and death struggle. Bending and wiping the bayonet clean on the stained coat of the man with the shattered head, and slipping it back again inside his boot.

Looking round in case the wharves hid any other rats, flicking out the spent cartridges, and reloading with the speed that came from years of long practice. Listening, senses straining for anything out of the ordinary.

But there was just the sullen noise of the fog-horns, echoing around the harbour of New York, reverberating about him, until it seemed as if the whole world was filled with wreathing mist and the boom of the ships.

It was full dark, the light having failed utterly during the brief scuffle. A scuffle that left two men dead on the dock and the third weaving and bobbing gently beneath the water, his hair like fronds of weed about the bloodless face and the staring eyes.

Only when he was sure that there was no further threat to him did Jed Herne turn to the motionless body of the young girl. She lay a few paces from the splintered edge of the wharf.

'Becky.'

He knelt down, feeling the damp through his trousers, lifting her head, and cradling her in his arms.

'Rebecca. It's me. It's Jed.'

Her head would have flopped back if he hadn't been holding it, and her eyes were shut. He could feel that she was still breathing, a faint pulse fluttering in her neck confirming that she was alive.

But there was blood around her nostrils, and trickling from the corner of her mouth. He wiped it away with his fingers, wondering if a stray bullet had hit her, or if one of the thugs had injured her.

'Becky! Can you hear me? Come on, Becky!' He felt the chill of utter desperation and loneliness, dropping his voice to a whisper. 'Becky, my love. Please, Becky. Please, my dear.'

The eyes fluttered and blinked up at him, barely visible in the gloom, and the corner of the lips curled up in an attempt at a smile.

'Jed . . . I must have . . . my chest hurts so and . . . and I want . . . cold . . . very cold . . .'

'I'll carry you. We'll get a cab and then we'll soon be good and warm. Come on. Up we go.'

Again he was shocked at her lightness, more like a child of seven than a grown girl of sixteen. Her head nestled against his shoulder and he stood up, smiling down at her.

Her eyes were closed again.

So he walked off the dock, towards the hotel, leaving the deaths behind him and carrying life with him.

Sweeping across the Hudson from the Jersey shore, came the first flakes of snow.

Chapter Three

The Grand Central Hotel was shrouded in snow by the time that Herne had got the semi-conscious girl back there. The cabs were nearly all off the mean streets, and it was a stroke of luck that he saw one wending its way home through the bitter weather. The driver refused to take them, and Jed was forced to draw his Colt to convince the man that it was urgent.

Their rooms were on the seventh floor of the new hotel, overlooking Broadway, with side views of the junctions of Bleecker and Amity Streets. Jed had booked in there simply because he had heard it was the biggest place in New York. The decorations alone were said to cost better than a half million dollars. A dining-room so vast that six hundred people could sit down and eat in great comfort and luxury.

Since there was still money left over from the last job he had done there seemed no reason to Jed not to spend it on the best. For Becky.

There was even a doctor kept on the premises, just for the benefit of the guests. At a price, of course. He was a young man. Very brash, very confident.

Becky was sleeping when he arrived, brandishing a small black bag, more interested in what Jed's relationship was to the girl than in what was wrong.

'I expect it's just tiredness. Or a touch of trouble with heavy menstruation,' he said.

'I heard of a lot of things, but never monthly bleedin'

from the mouth,' said Jed, feeling the red anger beginning to rise. Fighting to control himself.

'From the mouth, you said, Mister Herne?'

'Right.'

'A lot?'

'Enough.'

'You do know ... pardon me for asking this, but you do know a little about blood? Only I believe you are a cowhand or something.'

Herne clasped his fingers tightly together to stop himself busting the young man in the mouth.

'I seen a lot of dead, and a lot of dyin'. I know about blood.'

There was such venom in the voice that it finally penetrated the thick skin of the doctor and he took a step backwards as if he had been physically threatened.

'Now, now, Mister Herne. You and Miss Herne are ...'

'Miss Yates! She is my adopted ward.'

'Please. Keep your voice down. It is better for her to sleep and you call me as soon as she wakes. It is now nearly ten o'clock, but I shall be on call through the night if you require me.'

After he had gone, Jed walked silently into the girl's bedroom, looking down at her sleeping face. Seeing how young and vulnerable she was. The skin stretched tight over the cheeks, the eyes closed, though he could see the lids moving as if she was having a bad dream.

Acting on an impulse that he didn't even try and think about, Jed bent over the bed and touched his lips to Becky's face, kissing her as softly as a butterfly alighting on a leaf. She stirred in her sleep and moaned quietly, her fingers moving as if she was trying to touch something that lay just beyond her reach.

Herne sent down for a bottle of liquor and settled in a

deep chair at the side of the room, leaving on the solitary light set in the wall alongside the door. Dozing in the pool of yellow that it cast on the floor, just touching the corner of a framed print of a sailing-ship beating around Cape Horn in the teeth of a gale.

When she cried out, he woke up immediately, his hand dropping from force of habit to where his gun would have been, if he hadn't taken it off and left it on the small table by the side of the untouched bed in the other room.

'Jed. My throat! Oh, Jed . . . Jed!!'

The cry became a scream, even before he had powered himself from the chair to stand by the bed. He reached out and turned up the gas-light over the bed, looking down at the frightened face.

'What is it?' he asked anxiously.

She struggled to sit up. He reached down to help her, with an arm under the shoulders, bringing her to a more upright position.

'Drink. I have to . . .'

The suite of rooms had a private bathroom, and it took him only a moment, after shaking his head to clear away the mist of sleep, to reach a glass and fill it with water. Walking quickly back with it, ignoring the drops that he spilled on the carpet.

For a nightmare moment he thought that Becky was being attacked by an invisible creature. Her hands were at her throat, and she was fighting for breath, her face red with the effort, eyes starting from her head.

'Jed!!' she managed, as he brought the glass to her, then the eyes rolled up in the sockets, and she fell backwards, banging herself on the headboard.

Herne put down the glass and tried to help her up again, but as he did so a torrent of blood vomited from her open mouth, splattering all over the white sheets and the thick blankets. Pouring out like a river of crimson, soaking through her cambric nightdress, running over her fingers, and dripping to the floor.

'My God! Becky!'

For the first time that he could remember, Jed was helpless. If it had been a bullet wound, then he'd have known what to do. Bandage it up. But what could a man do when there was no wound, and the blood came from inside the throat?

The pendant around her neck swung loose, clotted with gouts of blood.

It was obviously a question of sitting and holding her, watching her die, or trying to get help.

The doctor was in the room within eight minutes. Eight of the longest minutes that Jedediah Herne had ever known.

By the time that he appeared, still rubbing at his eyes, the bleeding had slowed, and Becky was lying more quietly, half-moaning and half-crying. Jed had wiped most of the blood away from her face and mouth, trying to swab it clean with heavy towels from the bathroom, throwing the crimson rags into the bath.

'It has been what we of the medical profession call a massive haemorrhage from the pulmonary region,' pronounced the young doctor, after he'd examined Becky and given her a potion to help her to sleep.

'What the Hell do the medical profession intend to do about it?' snarled Herne angrily. 'We have to be moving west in a couple of days.'

The doctor turned to look at him, and there was genuine concern and sadness on his face.

'I am truly sorry, Mister Herne. I thought all along that you were aware of what the situation was and that you were keeping it concealed from the girl to save her from unnecessary distress.'

It was as though a great hand of icy steel had reached out and gripped Jed by the heart.

'What do you mean?'

'Come. Outside the room in case she can still hear us, Mister Herne.'

Gently, the doctor took the older man by the arm and led him from the room that smelled heavy with the sickly odour of spilled blood.

'Sit down.'

'I guess that I'd maybe rather stand, if'n you don't mind.'

The young man nodded. 'Very well. I will put it as best I can, Mister Herne. The girl is suffering, and has been suffering for some years, from a disease of the lungs. A form of wasting illness where the tissue of the body is destroyed. Often wetness and exposure to wind and cold can make this worse.'

'What? What are you saying?'

'A great German man of medicine named Robert Koch has very recently discovered a bacillus . . . that is what causes such an illness . . . and it is called tuberculosis.'

'Tuberculosis?'

'That's right, Mister Herne.'

'Come on, Doc. You're not goin' to keep puttin' it off. I'm her . . . her only relative. I have a right to know how long it'll be before she's better.'

The doctor didn't reply immediately, walking to the window, and pulling back the drapes, looking out over the sleeping, white-shrouded city. Replying without looking at Herne.

'That is precisely it, in a nutshell, Mister Herne. Rebecca Yates is *not* going to get better. The condition is too far advanced.'

'What are you . . .?'

'Rebecca is going to die.'

'Die!'

'Quietly. She will die, in my estimation, within the next twenty-four hours. Another haemorrhage like that last one will undoubtedly kill her, and I believe that it will not be long.'

Jed Herne took a deep breath, forcing air into his chest until it hurt. Saying nothing.

'Mister Herne. I can get you a skilled nurse, or I can stay. It will all be billed to you on . . .'

'Get out of here.'

'I think that it would be better if I were . . .'

'I'm grateful to you, and I believe what you say. So if there's nothing that can be done, then I'll stay with her. If I need you, then I'll call.'

'Very well.'

'Doctor?'

'Yes, Mister Herne?'

'She won't . . . you know . . . won't suffer when it comes, will she?'

The young doctor shook his head. 'The worst of the pain is already over for her. Rebecca will be very weak when she wakes.' He paused. 'If she wakes.' He spoke with an air of finality.

'And there's nothing you can do?'

'I'm truly sorry. There's not a thing that I or anyone else can do. I'll be ready if you need me.'

As he went out Jed said quietly: 'She's very young. Very young.'

But the doctor didn't hear, closing the door silently behind him. Leaving Jedediah Herne alone with Rebecca.

Somehow, cramped in the chair, Jed Herne slept. Fitfully, his rest disturbed by any change in the girl's breathing, his mind ravaged by dreams of the past.

A young girl, with Becky's face, running screaming from the blazing ruins of Lawrence, her back streaming fire like a bridal veil of red and yellow and orange.

Wandering through a great brothel, with a high vaulted roof, peopled by men and women from his past. All of them dead.

Just before dawn he woke, but Becky still slept. She was quieter now, her breathing less harsh, though Herne saw the traces of new blood about her lips.

He drew the drapes again, shutting out the glaring whiteness of the snow over New York. Great flakes still blew lumpily past the windows, torn apart by the rising wind.

A whiteness that was reflected in the clean sheets that the manager had sent up. Jed had changed the bed himself, rejecting any offer of help, tenderly moving the frail body of the girl.

A little of the old blood smeared the sheets, mixed with the startling brightness of the fresh blood.

Images that Herne took with him again as he slipped into a restless sleep, tangling with the memories of the way he had found his wife.

'Louise,' he said, unaware that his lips had even moved at all.

In his dream he relived that cold morning near Tucson. It had been bitterly raw, his breath frosting the air as he woke. Snow outside their cabin. Deadly white.

White sheets cold and empty at his side.

Like a new land viewed from the highest peak of a range of mountains.

Unsullied.

Except for where his wife had lain that lonely night, far on her side of the bed.

There the white was dappled and clotted with brown.

Dark brown that was still red in places where the blood hadn't dried.

In his dream, just as he had two years back, Jed found himself walking towards the barn, where the door stood open, a light wind tugging at it, making its hinges creak.

Knowing what he would find inside.

The green dress.

The overturned box.

The ray of pale light gleaming off the golden wedding ring.

Louise.

Louise.

'Louise!!'

'Jed.'

Half-waking, he staggered to his feet, peering round the room to see who had spoken.

Becky was watching him.

'Hello, Jed.'

'Becky. Did I waken you?'

'No. I was kind of dozing. I feel awful tired, Jed. I recall a lot of blood.'

'Surely. Coughin' like you were doing. It strained something in your throat, the doctor said.'

'I'll be all right?'

'Sure. Right as rain. We'll be off out of New York in a couple of days. Get you on your feet and smarter'n a lick of paint.'

But she was asleep again.

The doctor came up shortly after six, and took her pulse, checking her breathing, and feeling the heat of her brow.

'How is she?'

He shook his head. Looking at the girl, making sure that she couldn't hear.

'She is sinking, Mister Herne. All the parts of her body are, as it were, packing up their tents ready to depart.'

'When?'

'I think that she will probably live through the day. It is odd how the human body can cope when there is light in the world. But in the dark watches of the night, it becomes harder. If there is no further major haemorrhage, then I will be surprised if she lives through to see another dawn rise over this city.'

So he left them, urging Jed to try and snatch a little rest, putting a small brown bottle of the quietening medicine on the table.

After he had gone, Jed sat wearily in the chair by the bed, burying his head in his hands, suddenly feeling all of his thirty-nine years. And then some. Trying hard to recall the words of any prayers he might have heard. Finding that his mind had gone blank on him.

There was a rustling from the bed, and he looked quickly up to see that Becky was staring at him, her face pale as chalk.

'I wasn't asleep, Jed.'

'What?'

'I heard what the doctor said.'

'Now you mustn't think that he . . .'

'I know I'm going to pass on to the realms eternal, Jed. And I shall see Mama again. And dearest Louise.'

'It may not be . . .'

She shook her head. 'Don't fret for me, dearest Jed. I beg you. I have been unhappy for so much of my life that it is a relief to know that it will so soon be ended and I shall find peace.'

'If you rest up, Becky, then maybe we can get you well enough for a trip out west again. Like we said.'

She reached out for him, and he took her hand, feeling it lighter than a fistful of thin, dry twigs.

'I have loved you so much, Jed. You know . . .'

She stopped, and looked away from him, towards the window.

'What?'

'I thought for a time, in a silly, girlish way, that one day you and I might . . .'

'Might what, my dear?'

'That I might take the place of Louise in your heart and that we might marry.'

Jed felt as though his heart would break with the pain of her words, blinking away the tears that had gathered at the corners of his eyes.

'Don't talk. You'll make yourself cough.'

'No. I have been thinking while I lay here. I believe I knew that I would soon be gathered into Heaven, Jed. I must speak of what I would so like.'

'Anything.'

'I would so like to be laid to rest with Mama and sweet Louise.'

Rachel Yates and Louise Herne were buried together, in a plot of land that lay where their spreads had joined, near to a small stream, with a view far out over the plains to the distant hills beyond Tucson.

'If that . . .'

'I don't think that there will be any "ifs" about what is to come, Jed. Please promise me.'

Her fingers of her free hand played with the pendant around her neck, now cleaned of the blood.

Jed nodded. 'I'll do everything I can, Becky. You can be sure of that.'

The grip of her fingers on his broad, calloused hand relaxed, and for a moment he thought that she had gone, but her chest still rose and fell. She had once again drifted back into sleep.

Throughout that long day, Jed Herne sat and watched as life ebbed from the young girl. The only person on the face of the earth for whom he felt any shred of affection, and now an uncaring God was taking her from him. To leave him to walk alone.

Twice she recovered a little, and sipped some water to ease the dryness of her lips, but the effort made her cough, bringing flecks of blood. Each time, she seemed that much weaker.

The doctor looked in on them several times, each time shaking his head helplessly. Hardly talking. Seeing that the tall silent man needed no words.

Night came again, bringing an end to the snow. A flaming crimson sunset bathed the stone jungle in a warm light, flooding through into the hotel room where the girl lay dying.

At full dark, Becky woke again, and even seemed to be rallying briefly.

The doctor came, and examined her, walking out into the other room, followed by the unshaven figure of Herne.

'It is nearly done, Mister Herne. I have seen this false spark of vitality before. It is always followed by the end. You must prepare yourself for the worst.'

'Doctor,' replied Herne gruffly, 'I've been prepared for the worst every damned day of my life.'

'It's very dark here, Jed. Could you turn up the light for me?'

He reached up and twisted the little brass tap, letting the gas hiss through, brightening up the large room. Becky seemed very small in the big bed.

'How do you feel?'

'I'm weak, Jed. Very tired, as if all I want to do is close my eyes and rest.'

He was unable to hide his feeling that this was the end, and she saw him.

'Dear Jed. Don't weep for me. I should weep for you, leaving you here all alone. I shall be well enough with Mama and with Louise. She'll be pleased to see that I am still wearing this pendant. You won't take it from me, will you, Jed?'

'No.'

'Come sit with me, and hold me. I've always wanted you to hold me, and never dared ask you. I do love you, Jedediah Travis Herne. You know that, don't you?'

He nodded, not trusting himself to speak, afraid that he would break down at a time when she most needed reassurance and strength.

'I'm truly not frightened. Well,' she hesitated. 'Perhaps I am a little bit. But I mustn't complain. I have seen much of the world. Had a deal of happiness not to mention the fine adventures we had.' She stopped as a thought struck her. 'Jed?'

'What is it, Becky?'

'Whitey?'

'What about that old son of . . . what about him?'

"Will I meet him again, beyond?'

'I always reckoned that Whitey Coburn was the surest bet a man could make to go down and not up. But, things are mighty strange. Maybe you'll see him somewhere's around.'

'I'd like that.' She laughed, the smile turning into a coughing fit that left her weak and panting.

'Try and rest, Becky.'

'No. It is getting most awful dark, Jed. I used to be powerful scared of the dark when I was little. Shall we sing?'

'Maybe it's better not.'

'Perhaps. I'd have greatly been pleased to have a verse or two of "We'll Gather At The River". It was one of my favourites, and one of Louise's also.'

Almost without her noticing, Jed saw that her breathing was slowing down, like an engine that has been worked that little while too long.

'I wish that I could have been loved. By a man. I'd have liked that, you know. That sounds rather wicked of me, but I hope that Jesus understands.'

'I guess he will, Becky.'

He held her hand tighter, trying to prevent the frail spirit from leaving him, but her voice was becoming quieter.

'I know that Mama would have been shocked, Jed, but I surely wish that you would have laid with me. You don't think Louise would have minded?'

'I guess not. If it had been anyone, then I figure she'd have been pleased that I chose you. I'd have liked it too, Becky, but things . . .'

He couldn't go on.

'Things didn't turn out that way. She'll be sorry that you go on with the killing, Jed, but I understand.'

'It's all I can do. All I'm good at. All I truly understand.'

'I know. Honest I do. Jed, I'm turning cold. Hold me tight against the chill.'

He reached round her, folding her thin body close to him, feeling the tears coursing down his cheeks, knowing that it was nearly over.

'Remember to lay me in Tucson, Jed. With the others. Promise.'

'I promise, Becky.'

'I'm going to think of the good times, Jed. Think of being young and free and running through the pastures in summer, with the sun on my shoulders and the earth warm beneath my bare feet. That's a good thing to carry with you. Best there is.'

The mist was rising off the rivers of New York, closing round the hotel.

Her left hand was tight in his, the other hand holding the small pendant.

'I thought it didn't seem fair, but now I don't mind. It's being young, and leaving so much undone, Jed. But . . . I guess there's no value in grieving. Jed?'

'Yes, dear Becky?'

'Will you say the Lord's Prayer with me?'

'Of course. You lead me. Seems a long time since I set my tongue to it.'

With him saying the words behind her, Becky lay back in his arms and closed her eyes, her voice now so quiet that it scarcely disturbed the air in the room.

'Our Father, who art in Heaven. Hallowed be Thy name. Thy Kingdom come, Thy will be done, on Earth as it is in Heaven.'

Louise used to say the prayer each night before joining Jed in bed, and the rich words flowed back into his mind, his voice rising above Becky's.

'As we forgive them that trespass against us. And lead us not into temptation, but deliver us from evil.'

Her head was pressed against his shoulder.

'For Thine is the Kingdom, the power and the glory. For ever and ever. Amen.'

They had started the prayer together, but he finished it alone.

Jed Herne was quite alone.

Chapter Four

'Damned good job the weather's as bleak as this, Mister. Else this wouldn't have been taken.'

Herne looked up at the garrulous conductor, his face set like stone. The trip out to St. Louis had taken two days. Leaving New York had taken a further two days. Jed had been touched by the collection that had been taken up among the guests of the Grand Central Hotel to provide an expensive funeral for Rebecca Yates. Better than four hundred dollars had been raised and Jed had been able to use it.

Despite his promise to the dead girl, he hadn't realized just what he was taking on in trying to get her back to Tucson, to rest with her mother and with Louise.

The mortician had been fascinated with the task.

'Of course, my poor dear Sir, we do sometimes receive some most unusual requests. A gentleman who wished to be laid to rest in a double coffin with a dressmaker's dummy at his side. A sporting lady who required that she should be laid to rest seated in her favourite buggy. That was *very* costly. And I have had several departed who have wished for their remains to be buried at sea or in some even stranger places.'

He had rubbed his kid gloved hands together at the happy and costly memories, while Jed had stood still, looking through the large window, reading the ornate Gothic golden lettering backwards. Hoping the man would be quick and tell him what he wanted to know.

'One man, and I must preserve his name to avoid any impropriety with the family, had a long-standing relationship with a street-girl in Harlem. He wished his coffin to be built into the frame of a bed, so that she could carry on her trade on top of him, as it were.' He smiled. A tactful smile that landed on his mouth like a layer of fine, grey dust. 'Of course, we were unable to provide that particular service for him.'

'I don't see why not,' snapped Jed. 'But I just want to know how much. For the coffin and for . . . for preparing Becky for it. And the rail fare to Tucson. I can take it from there.'

A lot of scribbling with a long green pencil. The point broke and the mortician cursed softly, discreetly, reaching for a small knife and making it needle-sharp once more.

He was so thin and willowy that he looked as if a fresh breeze would carry him away.

'The cleansing and internal . . .'

His nerves strained by the sudden death of the girl, and with lack of sleep for two nights, Jed's hair-trigger temper was more than usually edgy. He half-drew the heavy pistol and showed it to the mortician.

'I don't want your damned details about what you're goin' to do to Becky. Just the money, you blood-suckin' son-of-a-bitch bastard!!'

'You talk to me like that and I'll call the law, Mister,' protested the young man.

'You call your sheriff, and you end up deader'n a beaver hat. Get on with it.'

With a chill, the mortician realized that this grizzled westerner actually meant it. That he would slaughter him if he didn't do as he was told.

The idea was rather exciting and he had to press his knees together to try and cover his arousal by this man's casual brutality.

'I'll do the best I can, Mister Herne,' he stammered, dropping his pencil deliberately so that he would have the opportunity to kneel down close by the older man's scuffed boots and worn pants.

'No details. Just the cost.'

'Fine. Even in the sort of weather you'll be having all the way West, we must still provide a sealed coffin. The railroads insist on it because of the way that the bodies tend to . . .'

Herne interrupted him. 'I know why they insist on sealed coffins,' he barked.

'Of course. Of course. That means good quality, and good quality is not cheap.'

Herne took out his watch, holding it flat in the palm of his left hand.

'You are in a hurry, Mister Herne?'

'No. You are. You're in a hurry to finish tellin' me what I want to know in just sixty seconds, then I start to push your face around a mite.'

'Oh,' quavered the mortician, torn between fear and excitement.

'Fifty-six seconds,' said Herne.

'Hundred dollars for pre-coffin work. Say, three hundred for the casket and sealing. I'll have to check shipping but I figure it'll be around another hundred to a hundred and fifty dollars. Through St. Louis then on the . . . let me see . . .'

'Union Pacific to Topeka, is the way I see it.'

'Surely. Then the Atchison, Topeka and Santa Fe Railroad south to El Paso.'

'And the Southern Pacific to Tucson,' finished Herne, flicking the watch away into a pocket of his jacket.

The final bill was five hundred and eighty-nine dollars and forty cents.

'I said this wouldn't have gone in summer, even with that sealing, Mister.'

The conductor on the Union Pacific pressed on, disregarding the silent stranger with the long hair, greying at the temples. Ignoring the tight set of the broad shoulders and the blank stare from the cold eyes, that looked as if they were one too many mornings and a thousand miles away.

'You hard of hearin', Mister?'

The eyes finally acknowledged him.

Eyes colder than the Sierra snows, that froze the man to the floor of the carriage. Froze his tongue to the top of his mouth, and turned his brain into ice.

'You got a job to do?' asked Herne, his voice flat and incurious.

'I . . . I guess so, Mister,' stammered the conductor.

'Then get the Hell away from me and do it.'

'Sure. Sure will. Right away.'

He stumbled quickly down the car, relieved to be clear and away with his life, breathing deeply to try and quell the sickness that rose in his guts at the memory of those eyes.

Jed Herne sat back in the dusty seat and looked out across the bleak landscape rolling by outside.

It had been hard. Dealing with the mortician, and the well-meaning folks at the hotel, but now it was over. He and Becky were both going on home, travelling West, following the pale winter sun.

The coffin was heavy. Polished mahogany. A neat plate in silver set into it. The name: Rebecca Yates. The date of her birth: 1868. And that of her death: just sixteen short years later.

He'd given her best dress to them for her to wear on her last journey. He kept the pendant himself to put on at the last moment, before the coffin lid was screwed down tight and sealed. Although it wasn't worth that much, it was a pretty piece, and some light-fingered thief in the mortician's might have taken a fancy to it. It wouldn't have been the value. It would have been the broken promise.

Herne had been shocked when he saw the girl that last time, in the soft lights of the chapel of rest, laid out in her pretty clothes. There had been too much rouge on the cheeks, and he'd angrily demanded that it was wiped off.

'Damn it! She's a girl of sixteen, not a Memphis whore!'

They'd hurriedly done as he asked, finally leaving him alone with her, for the last words.

They hadn't come easily, and they'd been private, secret words. That nobody would ever know. Not there. Not anywhere.

Not ever.

When he stood back, there were tears on his cheeks. Not for himself. Herne the Hunter had always made out and always would. Until the day that someone faster came along.

The tears were for the lost years for Becky.

He leaned over and kissed the girl gently on her firm, cold cheek, and then watched while the last rites of the sealing were carried out.

The baggage car had been nearly empty. Not a lot of stuff being shipped west in the middle of winter. Nor were there many passengers aboard.

After the change at St. Louis, things weren't any different. Nor, after a few hours on the Kansas Pacific, was there any change on the run south from Topeka.

Herne drank a lot and slept more. Folks on the train left him alone, figuring that the tall man with the mean face and the Colt strapped to his hip wasn't the sort to enter willingly into conversation.

Across the Arkansaw River in a freak blizzard that held them up near Dodge City for two and a half days until they could get the special train through with the big snow-plough on the front.

Past Trinidad and into the Territory of New Mexico. Another storm sent the train up the branch line into Santa Fe. Herne scarcely noticed the delays, soaking up the booze and laying out on the bench seats.

Snow on the line between Albuquerque and El Paso meant another day wasted. Money was running short, and there was still the actual burial to arrange. As soon as Becky was safe in the ground, Jed was going to have go looking for another bounty.

At El Paso they transferred to the Southern Pacific Railroad, and a few more folks boarded the train. Mostly making the long journey from New Orleans clean through to San Francisco.

That didn't worry Jed Herne. He found himself a seat and stretched out along it, waiting for the day's ride through Apache country to Tucson.

The end of the line for him.

The unusually bitter weather didn't concern him either. He simply tucked up the collar of his jacket and gripped the whisky bottle more tightly.

The train had only just lurched out of El Paso, with a clattering of wheels and its whistle screaming, when Herne realized that someone was watching him. He propped open one eye and stared across the car.

'Pardon me, sir,' said the stranger, 'but I feel that I know you.'

Jed shook his head. 'Guess not.'

The man opposite was around six feet tall, carrying better

than two fifty pounds around with him, a lot of it bulging out over a massive leather belt. On each side of the belt hung a Colt forty-five. A matched pair with ivory handles, Herne noticed.

Despite the guns, the stranger wore a tight suit of obviously Eastern cut, topped by a light brown derby hat two sizes too small. The face was round and honest. As far as you could tell. One of the most open-faced, likeable men that Jed Herne had ever met made a speciality of slitting the throats of young girls and drinking their blood!

You could never go far by appearances.

He was certainly persistent.

'I'm sure I do know you. Have you ever been up in Montana?'

'Yes.'

'Then it was there.'

'Guess not.'

'Ogden, in Utah?'

'Been there.'

'Then it . . .'

'No.'

The big man took off his hat and scratched his head, the movement opening his vest and revealing a small pistol in a holster under the left arm.

'I still think I know you, Mister . . .? I guess I didn't catch your name.'

'That's because I didn't throw it your way.'

'I hear you're the man travelling with the little girl's casket.'

'You heard right.'

'Kin?'

'Kind of. Takin' her back home to Tucson to be laid down with her folks.'

The man nodded. Rubbing his hands together and

blowing on them. 'Damned cold! I'll be glad when we get to the coast and I can get off and eat some good food and lay me between some warm blankets.'

'You on business?' Despite himself, Herne found himself drawn to the fat man's obvious good nature.

'Surely am. You hear of the Pinkerton Agency?'

'Eye that never sleeps? Sure.'

'I'm with them. Agent Lovell. Harry L. Lovell. I'm pleased to meet you, Mister . . .? Still don't seem to have your name.'

'I'm Herne. Jedediah T. Herne.' He reached out to shake the agent's hand, but Lovell sat still, lips set in a hard line.

'Jed Herne?'

'Yeah.'

'You wouldn't be the man they call 'Herne the Hunter', would you now?'

'I've been called that.'

Lovell leaned back, fingers unconsciously dropping to toy with the butt of the right-hand Colt. Biting his lip nervously, not sure where to look.

'I heard a lot about you, Mister Herne.'

'That figures, Mister Lovell. I heard plenty about me as well. Most of it lies.'

'You were the best. Then you got killed, I heard. Then, year or so back, the word came that you were back on the bounty trail.'

'I wouldn't argue with that.'

'Mind if I ask you what happened?'

'I mind.'

'Oh, I just wondered why you quit, and why you came back.'

'Keep wonderin', Mister Lovell. Just you keep on with that wonderin'. Now, if you'll excuse me, I could do with some sleep.'

'You . . . Pardon me for asking you this, but I wondered if you and me might even be on the same mission. That really would be something to tell the wife and kids when I get home to Tuscaloosa.'

'When I work, Mister Lovell, I keep that to myself. I seen men that talk a lot. Men with the brains of a fence post. Mostly dead men by now.'

'Sure. Sure, Mister Herne. I take your meaning there, indeed I do. Word to the wise, Mister Herne.'

The Pinkerton man was rubbing his nose and winking at Jed as if he was plagued with some kind of nervous tic. Leaning back in his seat, and easing his guts over his belt with a sigh of satisfaction.

Herne closed his eyes and tried to sleep, ignoring the other man's attempts to restart the conversation.

Lovell finally lapsed back into a muttered monologue.

'Herne the Hunter. God damn it, but that is really something to tell the boys. Herne. Knew Billy the Kid, they say. Best damned gun around. Damn it to Hell! Herne on this train with me.'

The monologue faded away and Herne finally managed to sleep.

When the train started to climb higher into the hills, halfway across the last leg of the long journey, Herne felt a hand tap his shoulder, and he woke to find the Pinkerton agent pointing out of the misted window.

'What the . . .?'

'More snow. Don't see that kind of weather much in these parts, ain't that so, Mister Herne?'

'Jesus. You woke me up to tell me that it's snowing! I don't give a sweet damn about it. Just as long as I can get to Tucson. Then I start over.'

'You never thought of joining up, Mister Herne?'

'Pinkerton's?'

'Surely. Regular money. Travel. Touch of excitement now and again.'

'I get all of that when I want it. It's not hard getting bounty work.'

Lovell nodded furiously, his treble chins bobbing with his enthusiasm. 'Bet you killed you a lot of men for money, Mister Herne?'

'Some. Most I killed 'cos it was the best way of stoppin' them killin' me.'

Looking round the quiet car, Lovell leaned forwards, dropping his voice to a whisper.

'Glad to have someone like you with me, in case things get tough.'

Herne was puzzled. There had been no armed guards on the train, and the baggage car had been more or less empty. So what was the fat man guarding?

'I guess I can trust you, Mister Herne, you and me being in the same line of business.'

Lovell was obviously bursting a gut to tell him his secret, and Herne couldn't raise the energy to stop him. Not even to tell him that it was a whole lot safer to trust nobody.

The line of the law was very thin, and out on the frontier it sometimes got so thin that it became invisible. Some of the biggest robberies in the last twenty years had been carried out by sheriffs, or deputies, or even by bounty hunters seeing a chance of better rewards by crossing over that thin red line.

'Yes, sir. The old eye that never sleeps is on the watch over something pretty damned precious. Not like gold or jewels. No bigger than this ...' He held his hands a few inches apart. 'But heavy. Real heavy.'

Herne nodded. 'Printing plates.'

If Jed had pulled a copperhead snake down his nose Lovell couldn't have looked more shocked.

'Jesus! How did you know that it's printing plates I'm

guarding?' A sudden look of suspicion. 'You sure you aren't in some manner involved in this, Mister Herne?'

'Mister Lovell,' replied Herne, wearily. 'If I was on your side I wouldn't be callin' it out to the whole world and its neighbour. If I wasn't on your side, then I'd have killed you by now.'

'Then how did you . . .?'

'Not gold. Heavy. The size. Has to be something worth a dollar or two. Must be printing plates.'

'Keep your voice lower, please, Mister Herne.' Despite the cold, Lovell was sweating. He looked round the car again, checking out that nobody was near enough to hear them.

Jed had already checked that out, as a matter of habit. There was a group of four men down the far end that interested him. The rest of the carriage was a scattering of ordinary-looking folks. Families. Children. Pair of women travelling together; probably a mother and daughter from their looks. A priest who had sat all the journey with his nose buried in a large Bible.

Nothing to worry about.

But those four men . . .

One looked Mexican, with a small moustache. Two others could have been cowhands, but you didn't often see range boys carrying their guns as low on the hip as they did. The fourth man was dressed in a black cutaway coat with pearl buttons.

They didn't talk much, but when they did it was with heads together. The Mexican kept wiping the steam off the window with his sleeve and staring out. Herne watched them, wondering what they were plotting.

Wondering about those printing plates.

'We have an agent in Tucson, Mister Herne, and I have to check the plates with him when we get there. A Government official will look them over before I take them on the rest of the way to San Francisco. If they fell into the wrong hands, well, I just shudder to think . . .'

And he did shudder, his broad shoulders quivering violently.

The priest across the aisle looked up curiously at the juddering of the huge frame, then went back to his quiet meditations.

The train rolled on westwards under grey skies, across a barren and empty land, riven with great hills.

It became colder and colder.

It was growing darker as well as colder, with night following the slow-moving train from the rear, closing in on it like a cloaked band of Apaches, bringing the conductor along the three carriages to light the small lamps. They gave off a smokey smell of oil which mingled with the damp, chilled air.

The bottle was empty and all Herne wanted to do was sleep again. In the morning they would pull into the station at Tucson, and there would be a lot for him to do. He nodded a goodnight to the fat agent opposite him, also giving a half smile to the priest who was looking at him over the top of the Bible.

Most of the passengers were sleeping or readying themselves for sleep, except for the group of four men at the far end of the car. They were playing a quiet game of poker, the money chinking on the seats as they placed their bets.

'Goodnight to you, Mister Herne,' said Lovell, stifling a belch with the back of his hand.

Jed closed his eyes.

'First person to move gets a bullet through the head.'

The voice was quiet. Controlled. Only just loud enough to

carry the length of the car. It woke Jed up and his hand was on its way after the Colt before he even opened his eyes, checking out what was going on.

Three of the four men were standing near the end of the carriage, where they'd been playing cards. The fourth man had disappeared. All three men held pistols, covering everyone.

There wasn't a lot of fuss. One of the women gave out a half-scream, but the rest sat quiet and easy, cowed by the threat of the guns.

Jed glanced behind him, wondering if he could make it to the door out to the baggage car. Deciding that they could gun him down before he was able to move three steps. Also deciding that it really wasn't his fight. From what Lovell had been saying, Herne guessed that the bandits must be there for a purpose. And that the purpose might be connected with those valuable printing-plates.

'Someone's talked,' whispered the Pinkerton agent, his face taut with horror. Fingers working like he had something sticky on them, and couldn't work out a way to get them clean. Rubbing, edging nearer the butts of the matched pair of pistols.

Herne wondered if he really would have the nerve to make a play under the threat of the three guns. Eyes flicking around to see if there was any other way out. The priest saw him and shrugged helplessly, the Bible closed on his lap.

'I can't. Just can't,' said Lovell. 'You with me?'

Herne didn't reply.

Didn't have to.

'Men up and let the guns go. Real slow and easy.'

It was the tall man in black speaking, smiling over the barrel of the Colt in his right hand.

Behind him the Mexican was still peering worriedly out of the window.

'Cal? We gonna make it up the trail into Pinaleno Mountains in this weather?'

'Shut up, Diego. We get to the trestle and then we can make it easy up to the north.'

Herne listened, vaguely interested to hear them discussing a region he knew well. They were making for the Pinalenos range. There was only one trail off a trestle bridge, and it led to a disused mining camp. He kept that to himself, figuring they wouldn't take kindly to anyone knowing exactly where they were headed.

Seeing his one chance slipping away as the men were disarmed, Lovell made his move. Diving sideways with a surprising speed for a fat man, he drew both pistols, and rolled left behind the seats, close by the priest.

Jed was puzzled when none of the bandits made a try for the agent, simply standing there as if they were waiting for something further to happen.

The priest leaned forwards, touching the kneeling Lovell on the back with the Bible, in a strange gesture, almost of blessing.

There was a muffled explosion, and the end of the gold-blocked book seemed to explode in a haze of black powder smoke. The fat man toppled forwards, and lay still, blood trickling from a hole just below his left shoulder. The cloth of his coat smouldered from the contact burn.

Herne didn't move, knowing that his own life hung by a thread. The priest looked at him and shrugged his shoulders again.

'I guess that's what they call a book of revelations, Reverend,' said Herne.

Chapter Five

The missing fourth bandit had worked his away along on the roof, reaching the cab of the locomotive and stopping it by the simple expedient of shooting the driver dead and pulling back on the main brake.

As the train lurched to a halt, Herne squinted out of the side window and saw that they were stopped near the end of a trestle bridge.

'Stand still,' snapped one of the robbers, menacing him with a gun. Herne's own Colt lay with the rest of the passengers' weapons, at the feet of the man in the black coat with the pearl buttons.

The robber in priest's clothing was kneeling by the side of the dead man, tugging off his gunbelt and removing the derringer from its holster.

Finally trying to close the staring eyes with his thumb and giving up when they persisted in springing open, to gaze sightlessly at the ceiling.

'You know what he did for a living, Mister?' asked the 'priest', looking up at Herne.

There didn't seem much point in pretending ignorance, so Jed nodded. 'Sure. He was an agent for the Pinkerton Detective Agency.'

'That explains it,' laughed the man.

'What?'

'Why I can't shut his eyes. Even dead he's still tryin' to live up to the old "eye that never sleeps" motto.'

The joke brought howls of laughter from the rest of the bandits, now herding their prisoners into the end of the carriage away from the pile of weapons.

Herne had already decided that he was going to just stand there and let it happen. He had no interest in the Government plates. Certainly not enough to risk his life for them.

But there was something about the robbery that made him uneasy. None of the robbers were making any effort to hide their identities. They used names casually as if they had no fears of any of the witnesses talking about them.

There had to be a reason for that.

A reason that Herne was suspecting when he saw the Mexican, Diego, looking down at the drop of three or four hundred feet to the dry river-bed beneath, and smile at one of his comrades, a wall-eyed man named George.

Jed caught the phrase 'fall like dry leaves', and had a strong feeling that it was the train and the passengers that were being talked about. If they had dynamite to blow the door of the baggage car, it would be all too easy for them to use a little of it to blow the bridge.

'You will all stay in this one carriage, folks,' said the leader of the robbers, Cal. 'You'll soon have company. Nobody tries anything and nobody finishes up getting hurt.'

When Herne heard the boom of an explosion, he hoped that they hadn't harmed Becky's coffin.

While they waited, night closed in around the train. There were twenty-seven adults and eight children in the carriage, guarded by the Mexican and by George. Cal, the priest, whose name was Luke, and Danny, the fifth member of the gang, were all outside. At least one of them had gone to fetch hidden horses; Herne could hear them whinnying in the darkness.

He suspected that it was Danny, as Cal and Luke had been in charge of the dynamite, handling the greasy yellow sticks with casual expertise. From the noise in the baggage car it appeared that they had been successful in blowing the door without wrecking the whole works. There was the noise of splintering wood as they systematically opened every box and case in the car, seeking what they wanted.

Herne was prepared to bet any money that they would reappear with the printing plates.

The door opened, and all eyes turned towards the man who entered. It was the bogus priest, Luke, and he was grinning from ear to ear.

'Got them. They was in a box marked as engineering tools. Cal's settin' the charges outside. George, go out there and I'll watch with Diego.'

'It's damned cold out,' moaned George.

'I go,' said the Mexican, tipping his hat courteously to the ladies.

'Right. Cal says not to bother with taking money or rings or nothing from these folks. We caused them enough trouble anyways.'

George laughed. 'Sure. Guess we don't want to call them no more trouble. Not at all.'

The broad wink that he gave the departing Mexican was enough to convince Herne that the plans of the bandits didn't include leaving any witnesses alive to talk about them. They were going to blow the bridge as soon as they were off the train, sending all their hostages on the breathless fall to the bottom of the chasm.

If it came to that Jed had already decided that he was going to risk a jump through one of the windows, hoping that he wouldn't plunge clean over the side of the bridge. But that would still leave a whole lot of innocent folks to die for nothing.

Maybe there would be a better plan turn up if he stood quiet and waited.

'Mister?'

The priest called out again. 'Mister? You. The old guy who was talking to the Pinkerton man.'

Herne realized the gun was pointing in his direction. 'Who, me?'

'Yeah. I feel I've seen your face before.'

It was one of the problems of being Herne the Hunter. Wherever you went you were likely to run into someone who knew your face. Now he thought about it, Jed had the feeling that he knew Luke. Luke . . .? Luke what? Then it came to him. Fort Laramie, where they'd been having some trouble with a few Arapaho bucks. Luke Barrell. That was it. Way back in about 'seventy. He'd been caught by a posse led by Herne on suspicion of running rifles to the Indians. Two of his accomplices had been hanged and he'd been lucky enough to get off, as there wasn't sufficient evidence to convict him.

Now he was staring at Herne over the end of a pistol. Finger white on the trigger. Trying to remember.

'What's your name, Mister?'

'Travis. Albert Travis.' Using his father's christian name and his own middle name.

'Travis. You ever been up around the Bozeman Trail through Fort Laramie?'

So he half-remembered as well. Herne shook his head. 'Nope. Never did get that far north.'

'I'm sure that I know you. And I'm damned sure that when I remember it'll be a whole cart-load of bad news for you. If I could . . .'

His thoughts were interrupted by a shout from outside, the words blurred by the rising wind. 'George, go see what they want.'

The robber went out, leaving the door open, so the cold air swirled through the carriage. There was an exchange of muffled bellows, and then George reappeared, shivering and slapping his hands together.

'Cal says they got what they wanted.' Then he dropped his voice and moved in closer to Luke Barrell. But Herne strained his ears and caught a mention of 'fuses', which was enough.

Death was very close.

Luke turned to the crowd at the far end of the carriage. 'George here says that there's a spot of trouble with our horses. I'm goin' out to take me a look. You all stand quiet now, and nobody gets hurt. As soon as we're away from here, there won't be anything to stop you walkin' away free as air.'

With a final stare at Herne, he turned on his heel and walked outside. Herne could hear his boots scraping on the wooden trestles, then a pause. Then a call up to George, who immediately looked at his pocket watch, licking his lips nervously. Finally, the noise of the feet moving away.

Immediately in front of Jed, a little boy was crying, his mother busy comforting another child. Herne bent down to pick him up, the movement as natural as brushing hair back from your eyes.

But when he straightened up, he was holding the honed bayonet in his right hand, concealing it behind the body of the bawling child. George watched him but didn't spot the concealed weapon, being more concerned with the watch in his hand. Herne wondered about the length of the fuse. Had to be long enough for them to get the horses well away, otherwise they might get spooked. And they had to give George time enough to get down and clear. But not long enough for the folks on the train to get suspicious or to put the fuse out on the dynamite.

'George?'

'What is it?'

'You sure you trust that Luke Barrell?'

'How the Hell do you know his name? Hey, he said that he knew you!' For a moment he looked out of the window into the swirling blackness as if he was thinking of calling back his comrade, then realizing the futility of it. But his face showed his worry.

'I did see him up in Fort Laramie, like he said. Better than ten years back. I saw him all right, and I'd rather trust a dying rattler.'

'What's that mean? You talk fast, Travis, or by God, I'll blast you where you stand, and take the kid with you!'

'He ran out on two of his friends there. Stood safe and watched them dancing on air with hemp collar tight round their necks.'

'Luke wouldn't . . .'

'Like Hell! He didn't need them, any more than they need you now, George. You're what I guess they'd call a mite expendable.'

'I'll . . .' The gun barrel wavered uncertainly, and there was another frantic look at the hands of the watch.

'They say to you to stay here on guard? Good old George, he's done well. Kept them folks in that carriage right until the big bang.'

'Mister, what are you . . .?'

The conductor on the train suddenly realized where Herne's words were leading. A realization that came swiftly to the rest of the folks. Herne knew there was a danger of panic and shouted above the screams and babble of voices.

'Hold on there! Keep calm. Let George do some thinkin' first.'

He had pushed his way to the front of the crowd, still gripping the bayonet in his right hand, so that he was only some eight paces from the bandit. Close enough to see the sweat that beaded the upper lip, despite the cold in the carriage.

The gun wavered. The little boy in Jed's arms had gone quiet and still, which he didn't want, and he pinched him to make him holler and wriggle again. Watching George like a hawk watching a jack-rabbit.

'Damn you, Mister! If you're wrong . . .'

'If I was you, George, I'd be a sight more concerned about what happens if I'm right.'

'Jesus! He wouldn't!'

'I'd wager with you, except we'd both be the losers, George.'

The final prod was enough. With a wordless yell, the man turned and took a step towards the door. Herne immediately dropped the child to one side, his right arm coming up and back, holding the heavy knife like a hatchet, by its hilt.

Throwing it with all of his power at the retreating figure. A woman screamed, and George began to turn back, sensing danger at the last.

He was too late.

Jed was able to take the heart out of an ace at twenty feet, so hitting George in the back at less than ten paces was like shooting fish in a barrel. Although he was just beginning to turn to face Herne, the point of the knife was already ripping through coat and shirt and skin and muscle, finally slicing through the walls of the heart.

'You bastard,' he said, before the impact of the throw sent him crashing back against the panelled door of the train. The gun was suddenly heavy in his fingers.

Bitter experience over twenty-five years had taught Jed the invaluable lesson that if your first blow doesn't succeed then you follow it up faster than smoke. His dive was a part of the throw, striking the bandit with his shoulder, hitting at the wrist holding the gun, sending it spinning to the dusty floor.

George fell backwards, the impact forcing the point of the slim bayonet so hard into his body that the ruby-tipped point emerged through the front of his chest, glistening in the light of the oil lamps.

'You bastard,' he repeated, making one effort to get to his feet, before he lay back, chest heaving. Fighting for the last few breaths, fingers tearing at the hem of his own coat in concentrated effort.

Ignoring him, Jed leaped to his feet, holding up his hand for silence, his blazing eyes controlling the carriage filled with frightened folks.

'I reckon they've dynamited the bridge. Men get your guns in case they're still out there. Women and kids off the train and off the bridge quick as you can. Don't wait for anything. Now!!!'

He shouted the last word to get them moving, pausing himself only to retrieve his own Colt and strap the belt on. Rolling over the dying man to tug out the bayonet, not even stopping to wipe it clean. Ramming it back in the sheath in his boot.

While the passengers fought their way off the car, climbing down into the murky darkness and stumbling along the narrow trestle bridge towards safety, Jed was kicking in one of the windows, scrambling through, tearing his sleeve on the way. Landing on the balls of his feet with the lightness of a cat, immediately scouring the night for the tell-tale glow of the burning fuse that he was sure he would find there.

There was a scream as one of the mothers tripped and fell sprawling, her body hanging between two of the railroad ties. The conductor helped her up, and Herne was aware of them all struggling to get off the bridge. He guessed that the explosive must be near the middle of the train, to make sure that it all toppled in when the bridge went.

So it had to be *somewhere* . . .

'There,' he said to himself, seeing the scarlet glint, getting close enough to hear the spluttering of the fuse. Throwing himself flat, Jed peered along between the still wheels of the stationary train, seeing where the bandits had taped a half dozen sticks of dynamite to the rods. The fuse sparked, a tiny yellow worm in the blackness, creeping its way towards the top of the explosive.

It was less than an inch away.

To reach it Herne had to crawl, spreading his body between the ties, hanging on the axle of the train, feeling the cold wind from the canyon far below tugging at his clothes.

A half-inch to go.

It wasn't possible in the time to get to the fuse and snuff it out. The only chance was to draw the bayonet and slice through the tapes. Angling his body painfully, stretching upwards, the hilt of the knife almost slipping through his sweat-slick fingers.

Feeling the blade cutting through the bindings, watching the glow of the fuse as it crawled nearer and nearer the dynamite, only a couple of feet from his face.

Suddenly, it was free, falling towards him, landing with a heavy thud on a cross-tie, one end hanging over the drop. The fuse had almost burned right through, and Jed knew it could only be a matter of seconds before it blew up, taking the bridge, the train, the passengers ... and him, with it. It was out of reach of his groping fingers. Wriggling like a landed salmon, Herne was able to change his grip on the wheel, moving the knife to his left hand, straining and just reaching the dynamite. Pushing at it with the point of the bayonet.

Knocking it clear of the trestles, watching it plummet to invisibility into the abyss below him. Panting with the effort, feeling perspiration stinging his eyes. His throat dry as sand.

He was immediately conscious of the night sounds. The

noises of the passengers still fighting their way off the bridge. Somewhere away in the distance he could make out the noises of horses, travelling fast. Up the trail that he knew would be leading them to the silver mine. Herne grinned to himself, seeing a chance to make some very easy money, telling the Government where the printing plates had been taken by the gang.

It was impossible to tell if the explosive reached the deeps of the canyon before the fuse finally ignited it, but the ensuing blast tugged at his clothes, and lifted the long hairs at the nape of his neck.

The air was heavy with the smell of the dynamite, and a thick cloud of smoke and dust billowed up all around him, making him cough.

'You all right, Mister?' called a voice from the further side of the bridge.

'Yeah. Yeah, I'm just fine,' he replied, replacing the bayonet once more in its hidden sheath.

Crawling out from under the train, standing up and brushing himself clean. Making sure the Colt was still safe in the holster, the thong keeping it secure. Walking steadily towards the yellow light that showed where the conductor had managed to lead the party of passengers to safety.

Joining them and shrugging at their praise for him, accepting a hug from one of the women, and handshakes from just about everybody.

All things considered, it hadn't been too bad. He'd killed one of the gang and he was going to be able to set the agents on them to recover the plates. What was best, he thought as he joined the guard and some of the men in walking to the baggage car, was that he had succeeded in avoiding any serious involvement.

He thought.

The door of the car was shattered to splinters, and the

inside was filled with open boxes and crates, broken by the robbers in their search for the plates.

By the light of the conductor's lamp, Herne was the first to see that Becky's sealed coffin had been ravaged. The body lay untouched, still wrapped in its scented winding-sheet.

But the pendant was gone.

Chapter Six

The train finally steamed into Tucson at a little after five o'clock that morning, with most of the children sleeping. The wrecked car was patched up with nailed battens of wood from the boxes, like a child's framework, shedding splinters all the way into the depot.

They were met by a handful of deputies, and a harassed Government agent, who first asked the train crew what had happened, then came wringing his hands to Herne.

'I'm Auden Jollye, Mister Travis.'

'The name is Herne,' said Jed, shortly, eager to get to a saloon and bath and sleep, then see to the burial.

Only then could he begin to think about going after the sons of bitches who had stolen from the dead. Stolen the pendant that had belonged to his wife. That should have been interred along with young Rebecca.

'Herne?' The agent was puzzled. 'I thought that the folks on the train said that . . .'

'I told them what I told them because . . .'

'Because what?' Although he appreciated that the little man in the dark suit had just been given a hell of a shock, Herne had taken an immediate dislike to him. He had the face of a quarrelsome rat, with a small moustache that looked as if it was hiding under his nose in the hope that his shifty eyes wouldn't notice it.

'Had a friend up in Oregon. Portland town.'

'Yes?'

'Got drunker'n a skunk one night.'

'I don't . . .'

'You will, Mister Jollye. You will. Took off every stitch of clothes and jumped clear in the middle of the biggest midden you ever saw.'

'Midden? Why . . .?'

'We asked him the same question. We asked him why he'd dived in the shit like that.'

'What did he say?'

Herne squinted up and down the street, seeing the backs of the passengers as they vanished off towards a saloon. Where he wanted to be.

'He said that it seemed like a good idea at the time.'

Herne turned on his heel and stalked away from the little man, leaving him fingering the scrub of hair beneath his nose and staring.

Wondering.

As he lay between the crisp, pressed sheets of the Tucson rooming-house, Herne thought back to the scene that had met his eyes in the damaged baggage car, standing there above the immensity of the deep ravine.

The coffin lay flat on the floor of the carriage, its gleaming lid ripped away at the screws by someone with a great deal of strength. The cold night air had been filled with an odd smell. Not the sweetness of death and corruption, but a bitter tang that caught at the back of the throat and stayed there. As he swallowed, Jed Herne could still taste it.

A chemical sort of taste, that he guessed must be something that the mortician had used to try and keep the body from rotting to a pool of liquid and stinking bones in the long journey. It had worked well, whatever it was.

The others had replaced the lid, but Jed had looked first,

making sure the pendant hadn't slipped down by the head, lodging among the silken cushions on the floor of the coffin.

It wasn't there.

Becky wasn't there. Oh, what she had left behind on earth after her spirit had been released was there. A cold, slightly wrinkled corpse, looking three times her age, with a white linen cloth bound around the head to stop the jaw sagging open and showing the mouth. The cloth shaded the eyes, and the oil-lamp hadn't been that bright, but Herne had seen them.

Hadn't been able to avoid them.

What was left of them.

They had gone milky, turning into opaque chips of watery stone, lying still and sour at the bottom of the deep sockets. Enigmatic and unfathomable. Perhaps they held a mystery. Jed didn't know.

Wouldn't ever know.

But the pendant . . .

That was something very different. They had tried to kill him, but that was nothing. They hadn't succeeded, and one of them was going to rest up on Boot Hill that afternoon. A lot of men had tried to waste Jedediah Herne, and nobody had made it yet. An attempt for the life of one of the gang didn't seem a bad exchange to Jed. But there were two other things to think about.

One was that he knew there would be a substantial reward for the missing plates. In the hands of what seemed a skilled and well-led gang, they could be worth a whole lot more than their weight in gold. And Jed knew where they were taking them. He figured they'd hide up the trail for a couple of days until the heat of the pursuit died down a little, then they'd move on.

Once they'd moved he'd lost them. He would have to go fast and hard.

If the money was right.

But in his heart Herne knew that he'd go after the gang for no pay. Just to get that pendant.

That was what mattered.

He finally dropped into a shallow and uneasy sleep, with the heart-shape of the rubies burning into his mind.

A red heart.

Red as blood.

'Mister Herne, I must say how very sorry I am. The sheriff here has only just told me who you are. So I came straight over.'

'Sheriff Wells?'

'Yes. He told me about Herne the Hunter. When I first heard the name I confess that it meant something less than nothing to me.'

'No reason why you should. I guess you spend a lot of time in an office holding up a desk, Mister Jollye.'

'Yes. I admit that I do.'

'You got the pallor. Only two sorts of men got that. Pen-pushers and convicts.'

'I don't see why you . . .'

'You wouldn't. Nor would you have heard of me out there in the Government, Mister Jollye.'

There was the hint of a smile, that made the face even more rat-like, baring a set of yellow teeth.

'No. Killers, thieves and assorted desperadoes are hardly in my line of business, Mister Herne.'

'They were in the way of the Pinkerton man, Lovell, were they not? There were those desperadoes, just waiting for the train. Waiting for your damned plates, Mister Jollye. Worth a lot, I guess.'

'You guess right, Mister Herne. Many thousand dollars in gold.'

'Lovell had a wife. Kids.'

It was a flat statement not a question, and the little Government man merely nodded. 'I believe so. I knew nothing about him.'

'I just wonder how much of your gold his widow and orphans think those plates are worth, Mister Jollye. You think on that.'

'I have no need to sit here and listen to you insult me, Herne.'

Jed stood up off the bed, buckling on his gunbelt. Towering the best part of a foot over Jollye, who recoiled a couple of paces in shock, nearly knocking over the wash-jug and bowl from the table near the door to the bedroom.

'I don't give a damn for you, Jollye, nor all the snivelling crew of you! I'm goin' after those bastards for my own reasons.'

'You know where they are?' butted in the agent, face lighting up with a faint gleam of hope that something might yet be saved from the disaster.

'You interrupt me again and you're goin' to be pickin' teeth out the back of your stiff collar, Jollye. Yeah, I guess I do know where they are, but, like I say, I go for my own reasons, to do my own job.'

'The plates.'

'You try makin' me an offer then I'll have me a think about it and decide whether it's one that I feel I can refuse or not. Now, if you'll excuse me, Mister Jollye, I have to go see if my Sharps rifle is safe off the train, and I have to go see a preacher about a buryin'. Good day to you.'

Herne retrieved the long buffalo gun from the depot and took it straight back to his room. After he'd dropped it off, he decided that it was time to go and get something to eat. At the top of the stairs of the rooming-house he caught a glimpse of the agent, bustling across the lobby. Jed pulled back quickly into the shadows, letting Jollye trot past him, before he continued down and out into the bright chill of the Tucson morning.

Crossing the trampled dirt of the street in search of somewhere to eat.

He was attracted by a sign that stated simply: 'Good, cheap food. Home cooked.'

The windows were sparkling clean and looked as if they'd been polished only that morning, and he could see inside that the tables were covered in stiff white cloths set with gleaming knives and forks. It looked the sort of establishment where he could eat well and in quiet comfortable surroundings. There was only one other person in there so late in the morning; an old man, with silvery hair, crouched over a steaming cup of black coffee.

Nothing escaped Herne's notice, and he was surprised to see such an old man carrying a handgun, tied low on the thigh in the classic position of the gunfighter. There was something about the set of the old man's shoulders that seemed familiar to Herne. Something from the past.

A silvery bell tinkled as he pushed the door open, to be greeted by the fresh tang of baking bread, mingled with the odour of dark brown coffee boiling on a stove. He inhaled noisily, heeling the door shut.

A red-cheeked girl in her late teens came through a curtain out back, rubbing flour from her hands on a spotted towel, greeting him with a pleasant smile.

'Morning. Nice day.'

'Looks that way.'

'What can I get you, Mister?'

'Some ham. Grits. Cornbread. Four eggs. Coffee. That'll be fine for a start.'

'How d'you like the eggs?'

'Over easy.'

'Fine. Sit down and make yourself comfortable. It'll take about ten minutes.'

Herne hooked a seat out with his foot, just to the right and a table behind the old man. Who had taken no notice at all of his entry, sitting slumped over his drink, chin resting on his left hand.

There was a sign over the counter that said: 'If you don't ask you don't get.' And another that said: 'If you don't like it then tell us.'

There hadn't been time to check that the action of the Colt hadn't been damaged by being dropped on the floor of the train, so Herne flipped the protective loop off the hammer and drew it.

Cocked the hammer gently back, with the soft triple click of the action.

'Dry-gulcher!'

The old man had caught the faint noise, and had reacted with amazing speed, diving sideways off the chair, sending the cup spilling. Reaching for the handgun on his hip with his right hand.

It would have been a brilliant piece of gunplay, and Herne might easily have found himself with a bullet in the gut from the old man.

Sadly, the fingers didn't obey the message from the brain and the Colt dropped from the hand, spinning out of reach.

Herne's own reaction was equally fast. He realized what was happening, and was on the edge of blasting the oldster across the room, when he saw the gun drop. He relaxed, easing back the hammer on his own Colt, meeting a red and angry pair of eyes, framed with silver hair, like a disarrayed halo.

'Bastard. Get it over with. Who sent you? Clanton? Who was it?'

'Take it easy, old-timer. Misunderstanding.'

'What?'

Herne raised his voice, finding it hard to believe that the old man had heard the gentle sound of the Colt and couldn't hear what he was saying.

'I said that you could get up and pick up the gun, Mister. My fault for taking out my own pistol.'

The raised voice brought the girl from the kitchen. She stood there, arms folded, looking at the strange tableau. The silver-haired man still sprawled on the floor, his gun a few feet from his outstretched hand. And Herne sitting at his table, about to holster his own Colt.

'Gramps! You just get up and stop actin' the fool like that or I'll send you up to your room.'

'Shucks, Ellie-May. I didn't mean nothing but this son of a bitch here . . .'

'Gramps!'

'Sorry, honey. But he drew on me from behind. Tryin' to backshoot me. Killer from Lincoln County is my guess.'

Herne stood up. 'I guess he's kind of right, Ma'am.'

'What?'

Still keeping a careful eye on the old fellow, Herne explained what had happened. The girl listened to him, and then repeated all of it to her grandfather, who nodded, and grinned, revealing a mouth that was high on gaps and low on teeth.

'Guess I owe you something, Mister,' he said, holding out his hand to be helped up.

Herne took it, yanking him to his feet, glancing at the girl in puzzlement.

She smiled, looking back to the kitchen. 'Must get back to those over easy eggs. Guess you're wonderin' how it is he don't hear what you say so well, and he hears me good and clear?'

'Yeah. And how he heard the Colt so fast?'

'Gramps used to be a gunman.'

'I figured that out. Seems like maybe I ought to know his face.'

'I think he . . . Land's sakes! Those eggs.' Shaking a finger at the old man who was stooping wheezily to pick up his fallen gun. 'Now you behave, Gramps. Or it's off to your room with you.'

She swept out, leaving the two men facing each other in a strained silence. Finally Herne gestured to the overturned table.

'Maybe we ought to pick that up.'

The words got through, and together they lifted the table up, setting the cloth square on it. Then stood there looking at each other, neither knowing what to do or say. Finally it was Herne who pointed to one of the chairs, pulling out the other and sitting down in it.

'Join me?'

'Sure. I guess I was a mite fast on slappin' leather, Mister.'

'Name's Jed Herne. Good to meet you.'

The brows wrinkled and there was obviously considerable effort going on inside the skull of the old man.

'Herne. Don't I know that name?'

'Maybe. I hear you were . . .' he changed his mind. 'Hear you use a gun. So do I.'

'That's right. You'll have to speak up Mister Herne. I don't hear so good since Wes fired off a derringer in my ear for a joke back in . . . way back . . . Herne? Ain't you the one they used to call the Hunter?'

'That's right.'

'I heard you was dead. Some trouble with the Cheyenne near Fort Phil Kearny up on the Powder.'

'That was the Fetterman affair. Back in sixty-six. Hell, I may be old but I was only in my teens then. Spunky kid full of fire and killin'.'

'Good to meet someone from the old times, Mister Herne. Real good.'

'Call me Jed. I don't know your name.'

The old man smiled. 'That's right.'

'I said I didn't know your name.' shouted Herne, trying to remember if he'd seen the face before. It was just an old man's face to him. Lined and seamed, a great jagged scar high up on the temple. Heavy scarring, with layers of skin folding in on each other. The oldster kept playing with it, letting his fingers touch it, then leap away as if they'd been burned.

'My name?'

Jed nodded, looking through the back and seeing that the girl was nearly ready with the meal.

'I'm Scotty. Scotty Mitchell. Rode with . . . what the Hell was his name? Damned how things slip away from you, Mister Herne.'

Again the finger rubbed at the old scar.

'Jed.'

'Sure. Jed.'

'You lived in Tucson long, Scotty?'

'Gramps has been with us nearly seven years now, Mister Herne.'

The tray the girl carried was well loaded.

The plate that she put in front of Jed almost creaked with the weight of the food. Fried eggs, jostling great slices of fresh ham. A white mountain of grits threatened to overwhelm everything beneath it, and the cornbread was piled so high a couple of pieces actually fell off the plate on to the cloth.

'I'm sorry.'

'That's fine. Miss . . . Mitchell, is it?'

'Surely is. I hear you saved the folks on the train, Mister Herne.'

'I did some.'

Scotty leaned forward. 'Herne the Hunter. That's where I heard of you. My name's Mitchell. Gunned down four men one noon in Lincoln, Nebraska. Or it might have been Juarez. Can't rightly recall. Must go out back. Pour me some coffee, Ellie-May. Seems I mislaid the last cup.'

He shuffled out, hand rising once again to that livid scar, vanishing towards the kitchen.

'If Gramps troubles you, Mister Herne, then I can easily get him . . .'

'No. Wouldn't dream of it, Miss Mitchell. That wound on his head?'

She sighed, pouring out two cups of brimming black coffee, strong enough to float a horseshoe on.

'That's much of it, Mister Herne. I know he's an old man, but he doesn't harm anyone. He really was a great shootist years back. All the tales we've ever been able to check on have been true. Even if they happened in a different town or in a different year.'

'I guess you could say that I've been in the same line of business as he has, for a good number of years, Miss Mitchell.'

'Mister Herne?' She was breathing a little fast, leaning towards him across the table. He noticed that a couple of buttons on her blouse had come open, and he could see the shadowed beginnings of her right breast peeping coyly out at him.

'Yes?'

'I guess you've been one of my heroes, ever since . . . well, since I can remember. It's so romantic, you being such a famous gunman. What a wonderful life you must have led. I surely wish you could tell me all about it.'

The invitation was there. No doubt at all about it. Herne had been propositioned times enough to be damned sure when a lady was laying herself right on the line for him. But she was very young, and he was going to be busy in the next few days.

'*Romantic*, Miss Mitchell?'

'You can call me Ellie-May if you like.'

'Why thank you. But let me tell you a little about the romance. The romance of running and hiding for months on end, jumping every time an alley cat knocks over an empty bottle. The romance of killing men. Seeing them die right in front of you, spewing up blood in your face. Gut-shot men taking three days to die screaming. Men the Indians have caught. That's damned romantic, Miss Mitchell. Seeing a horse with its belly ripped open by a Sioux lance, dragging its guts with it through mesquite and sagebrush until it falls over and can't rise. Why don't you ask your grandfather about the romance? Maybe he'll tell you what it's like to have to spend more time in cemeteries than in church. Buryin' friends and family. Havin' friends die in your arms, with no life left to come. And not damned much life behind them. Sure, it's real romantic.'

It was one of the longest speeches that Jed Herne had ever made in his life, and he had reached out and held the girl's arm to stop her moving away.

'You're hurting me, Mister Herne,' she said, face contorted with pain.

He let her go, gnawing his lip as he saw the great white marks where his fingers had bitten into her soft skin.

'I'm sorry. But I've lived it all my life, and the one thing that it is not, is romantic.'

'I understand that now, Mister Herne. I guess you must

think me pretty silly, what with having Gramps the way he is and all.'

'Maybe. But you don't ever learn anything if you don't get taught, Ellie-May. That scar on his head?'

'That's why I guess you never heard much of him. He got a bullet scraze there, way back. Before the War, we figure. That kind of made him a mite peculiar at times.'

'So long back?'

'We think so. Only he does get a mite confused about it. Said it was Mormons back in Iowa. After that he drifted around the country, living under a whole lot of different names. Most of them we don't know. But he lived by the gun.'

'You say he lived here for . . . how long?'

'Seven years about. Autumn of seventy-six it must have been. Course we saw him before then. Every year or so he'd pass by Tucson. I was born here. He seemed fine. A little odd now and then, but gettin' better. Talked about comin' home here to settle down.'

'So what happened? My, but this ham is the best I've tasted since I was last in Virginia, Ellie-May. Sure melts in the mouth.'

The marks on her arm were fading, and she smiled at him. 'Thank you, Mister Herne. Home killed, that hog was. Gramps and that scar, I was tellin' you about. We didn't hear nothing about him for couple of years, then he arrived looking like he'd been through the valley of death and come out the other side. Weighed about as much as me, and he looked like he'd aged ten years in two. Hair gone silver and that scar on his temple. Same place as the old bullet burn. Only much worse. Like someone had tried to split his head open for kindling.'

The coffee scalded his mouth, but Herne gulped it down, intent on the girl's story.

'Never found out for sure. What we think we keep kind of quiet about.'

'Why? A killing?'

'Kind of.' She hesitated. 'I'm sure I can trust you, Mister Herne.' There was the invitation again, and again Herne chose to ignore it.

'Go on.'

'He wouldn't talk much. His mind was much worse. Like you see him now. Confused and ramblin'. Like in a fever. Just said he'd been with some soldiers. For a ride. On the Yellowstone River. They'd been attacked, or they'd been attackin'. He never seemed sure. Then there'd been a whole load of Indians. More than the stars in the sky or the wheat on the prairies was what he said once. He was with a few of the soldiers, all the rest was dead. Climbin' up a hill to try and make a stand.'

They heard a door shut out back, and she spoke more quickly.

'Then more Indians came over the top of the hill and rode over them. One hit him with an axe and he doesn't recall another thing until he was in Butte with that scar and a headache he still has.'

'Seven years ago. On the Yellowstone. Soldiers being wiped out by an army of Indians.' Herne couldn't believe what the girl was suggesting.

'That coffee smells good,' said the old man as he rejoined them, smiling vaguely.

The girl shook her head in a warning at Herne not to mention what they'd been talking about and vanished out the back again.

The two men sat and sipped their coffee together in silence, while Herne looked at him. Looked at Mitchell's head wound. And wondered.

It had always been thought that there hadn't been a single

survivor seven years ago. When the Indians wiped out the soldiers up on the Yellowstone. Everyone knew that they'd been killed to a man.

With their impetuous leader.

Had Scotty Mitchell really ridden with Custer?

Conversation was hard. Half the time old Mitchell didn't seem to hear what Herne was saying, and the rest of the time he was rambling on about half-remembered events in half-forgotten places.

Every now and again a name would come up that Herne knew. Once it was even Billy the Kid. A story about Billy and Pat Garrett that Herne had heard Billy Bonny tell about himself, so he knew it was true. Scott Mitchell had surely been about.

Gradually, the story about the train came out. The name of Luke Barrell seemed to ring some kind of bell for the old man, but he couldn't hold it together and it evaporated into the mists of the black powder smoke of his past.

'Maybe I could help you, Jed?' he said, as Herne finished the meal and settled up the check with the girl.

'Gramps!' said Ellie-May warningly.

'Yeah, old timer. Maybe you could.'

'I'm still fast.'

'I saw it.'

'I recall the day that . . . that . . . what in Hell was I talkin' about Mister?'

'The train and the robbers.'

'Yeah. Course, I recall it, Jed. Lot of sons of bitches in that gang, didn't you say?'

'I did.'

'Well, if you want help, then let me know.'

The girl took the old man by the arm, trying to lead him towards the stairs.

'Time for your rest, Gramps.'

'I guess so. Remember what I said about some help, Mister Herne the Hunter.' The fingers rubbing at the knotted scar as if they could wipe it away.

'I'll remember that, Scotty. If I need you I'll just call you.'

'And I'll come a'running. Just like when old Two Moons chased me and gave me this wound.'

He vanished up the stairs, leaving Herne staring thoughtfully after him. Two Moons had been one of the leaders under Crazy Horse when Custer and his command was massacred. At the Little Big Horn.

Around seven years ago.

Chapter Seven

Jollye was waiting for him back at the rooming-house.

'Where on earth have you been, Herne?'

'I'll tell you this one more time and one time only, Jollye. You try crowdin' me like that and you'll end up with a broken face and no printing plates. You talk slow and easy to me, and we'll get along real fine. That understood?'

The agent drew a deep breath. 'Very well. I offer you my apologies, Mister Herne. Since I heard about the robbery, I have been almost out of my mind with worry. It is bad enough if criminal elements get hold of good counterfeiting plates. But to have the real thing . . .'

'Kind of like a strong-box that never gets empty, isn't it?'

Herne sat down on the bed and looked at the little Government man.

'We will pay you well for the return of those plates, Mister Herne.'

'I knew that before. Try me on something that's new.'

'One thousand dollars.'

'That's for just gettin' up on a horse.'

A sniff from the agent. 'Another thousand if you return with the plates.'

'Two now, and three more when I get back. I have to attend to a funeral. Buy a horse. Supplies,' Herne said firmly, brooking no argument.

'Very well. But when will you be able to start after them?'

'Tomorrow, if my plans go well. I figure the burial can be in the morning, so I could be away by noon tomorrow.'

'How . . . where . . .? Do you truly have any idea where they are?'

'Yeah.'

'You know?'

'I think I know.'

'You realize it is an offence to hold back on any information that might lead to the return of valuable Government property?'

'You realize I could bust you in the mouth and take a deal of pleasure in it?'

There was a silence in the room, taut as a bowstring, with both men eyeing each other warily. Much as Jed could use five thousand dollars, the pendant meant more to him. But Jollye was caught in a cleft stick. Much as he disliked Herne, if the big gunman really knew where those plates were, then it would be folly not to let him go after them.

'Five thousand dollars?'

'Five thousand dollars.'

'You bring the plates back to me, unmarked.'

'Unmarked?'

'Surely. If they are damaged then they are quite without value.'

'So if I don't get to bring them back in one piece, then it's fine with you if'n I mark them up so they can't ever be used.'

'Yes. Two thousand dollars for starting off. Three more if you get back to me with the plates, or irrefutable evidence that you have destroyed them.'

They shook hands cursorily, like men afraid of catching a contagious disease. The day was wasting away and Jed needed to arrange the burial of Becky out on the old spread with Rachel Yates and his wife, Louise. He felt a faint stirring of the small hairs at the nape of his neck at the remembrance of memories now past. Past, but not yet dead.

'I'll arrange to see you before you leave tomorrow, Mister Herne,' said Jollye.

'That'll be fine,' said Herne. 'Keep it to yourself about me knowing where those bastards are hid up. I don't want them coming into Tucson gunning for me before I can even get started.'

'Of course. I will have to wire my head office to the effect that there is good news on the way. I do hope that it turns out as good news, Mister Herne. I would hate to have spent two thousand dollars of Government money on a chase after a wild goose.'

'Like I heard a man say once, Mister Jollye; if you don't risk speculating, then you're never going to start accumulating.'

The agent left the room without another word.

On his way back from arranging the interrment with the local preacher, Herne bumped into the old gunfighter, sitting in a rocking-chair on the porch of the eating-house, whittling away at a piece of wood. Not seeming to carve anything in particular, just to pass the day along.

He looked up at Jed blankly, but then recognition came flooding to the wrinkled face and he leaped to his feet, setting the chair to squeaking.

'You're . . . don't tell me, Mister. It'll come along to me in just a . . . You ain't Ben . . . Nope, he got gunned down in a whore-house in Dallas.'

'Jed Herne.'

'What's that?' cupping a hand to his ears, and bending forward at the knees in a half-remembered gunfighter's crouch.

'I'm Jed Herne and you're Scotty Mitchell.'

A look of pure delight came to the hooded eyes. 'Damned right I am. You heard of me then, Jed?'

'Sure. Everyone from Juarez up to the Lakes has heard of Scotty Mitchell.'

'That's right. That's right. Sure is.' A thread of spittle hung white on his chin as he stood there nodding his head.

Herne noticed that the butt of the Colt on his hip was well-polished, and every few moments the old man's gnarled hand would drop to it, as if he was seeking reassurance that it was still there.

'I'll be seeing you, old-timer,' said Herne, preparing to walk back to his room through the gathering dusk. The funeral was planned for ten the next morning and he wanted to have time enough to get a good mount, and stock up on food and water for the trip into the Pinaleno Mountains.

'Wait on a moment, Mister Herne.'

The glaze had suddenly gone from the eyes and the voice seemed sharper. More biting.

'What?'

'I hear some things. Some things I don't hear good. But on account of my ears being kind of muzzy at the edges, folks talk in front of me where they might do well to hold their tongues. Can't abide that in a man.'

'Go on.'

'Yeah. Like Wes Hardin always said. If you come to shoot then get on with the shootin'. If you come to talk, then do it. Don't mix them up.'

'That's good advice, Scotty.'

'Sure is. I recall a couple of road-agents up in the north of Texas. Near Palo Duro Canyon, as I remember it. They had me dead to rights. Colder'n mutton. Sat there jawin' away at me as to how they'd been waitin' to bushwhack me on account of me killing their brother. Gave me time to draw and shoot them both out of their saddles. One was still talkin' when the bullet hit him. Sons of bitches.'

Seeing signs of the old man starting to ramble again, Herne took him by the arm.

'You had something to tell me, Scotty.'

'I did?'

'Yeah, you . . .'

'Sure. You and those fellows that took the train and the money plates.'

'What about them.'

'I know a guy over at the telegraph office and I heard him tellin' the bar-keep at the "Mother Lode" about how you been hired to bring it back. And that you knowed where them bandits took it.'

'He said that?' asked Herne, seething with a bitter anger that Jollye had been so indiscreet.

'Yeah. The bastard's a real drinker. Leans right up on the points of his elbows and bends the arm. After a couple he'll tell anyone about anything. He's about as much to be trusted as a treed grizzly. Talkin' of which did I ever tell you the time that me and . . . who was it?'

'Scotty,' interrupted Herne. 'You've been a whole lot of help. Thanks. But I've got to go.'

If the town oldster knew about his plans, then it might be that Tucson harboured friends of the gang. It wouldn't take that long to get a warning out. A fast horse during the night. They could be laying for him on the trail. Or even try and hit him in Tucson. He had to get away and think about it.

'Listen, Mister . . . Herne.' Scotty grabbed him by the sleeve of the coat. 'You don't forget now what I said. I'll be lookin' out for you. You want help, then you just give a whistle.'

Jed nodded. But Mitchell was looking anxiously at him. 'Remember, just whistle. You know how to do that?'

'I guess I do. Now you go in before it gets real cold out here.'

The old man grinned up at him, and shuffled away, in through the door.

Herne went back to his room to do some hard thinking and prepare himself for the next day.

Dismal weather greeted him when he rose the next morning. And even more dismal news. The priest was confined to his bed with a sudden cold and wouldn't be able to officiate at the burying until early afternoon in two days time. That would mean that Herne couldn't reasonably set off into the mountains until the morning after that.

Jollye was deeply concerned at the news, urging Herne to go ahead before the burial.

'No. If it's genuine, then not a lot of harm will be done. I have a feeling that maybe someone's got to the man of God and told him it might suit his health to rest up for a day or so.'

'Why?'

'I'll tell you that before I go. But I figure someone might ask the Sheriff here to keep an eye open for any strangers in town.'

'What are you goin' to do, Mister Herne?'

'I'm goin' to catch up on some sleep and do some buyin'. I'll see you in a couple of days.'

There it rested.

The priest duly recovered and they rode out to where Jed used to have his spread. A couple of local men followed on with the coffin on a wagon. The grave had been dug the day before, though the cold had made the ground hard.

Herne had pressed him on his 'illness', but the priest had coloured and looked away, muttering about something on his chest. It made Jed even more certain that there was pressure from someone in Tucson to keep him there for a few more days. If the gang wanted time to make their move, then that would have to happen. But, as Herne had explained to the anxious agent, he doubted that. If they'd made plans they wouldn't want to have to alter them on the chance of a bounty-hunter guessing where they were hidden.

No. It had to be that they planned an attack on him. Most probably on the trail.

'We brought nothing into this world, and it is certain we can carry nothing out. The Lord gave and the Lord hath taken away.'

The priest prayed, his voice raised against the curling wind from the east. The small coffin was ready to be lowered alongside the twin mounds where her mother and Jed's wife lay.

Herne wondered about just what it was that the Lord had given to Rebecca Yates. Dead at such a young age with so little of her life lived, and much of that young life filled with sadness and loneliness.

A thought that was strengthened as the coffin was lowered into the dusty earth with jerky stops and starts as the new rope round it screeched on the wood.

'. . . hath but a short time to live, and is full of misery. He cometh up, and is cut down, like a flower; he fleeth as it were a shadow, and never continueth in one stay.'

Jed stooped and picked a handful of dry sand, ready to cast it in on top of Becky's coffin. Hearing the priest as he spoke of the: 'Sure and certain hope of the Resurrection to eternal life.'

It rattled on the wood with a flat, hollow sound, and he

thought about Becky. Not about the wizened, rotting corpse that lay beneath his feet.

But the bright face of the beautiful young girl with the determined chin and the deep-set eyes.

'The grace of our Lord Jesus Christ, and the love of God, and the fellowship of the Holy Ghost, be with us all evermore.'

'Amen,' chorused the two grave-diggers, bending to pick up their shovels and fill in the black hole.

'So long, Becky,' said Herne, quietly. 'I'll get that pendant to you. I promise that.'

The priest came over to him, face set into the conventional lines of sympathy, only to recoil at the look of anger on the face of Jed Herne.

'What can be wrong, Mister Herne? Was the service not to your liking?'

'Surely, Reverend. I love funerals. All those last rites. In some cases it could be that they're last wrongs, wouldn't you say?'

'I'm afraid that I don't understand, Mister Herne. The ways of God are strange.'

'The ways of his servants don't bear too much lookin' at neither.'

The shovels scraped in the earth, filling up the grave, and sealing in Becky. Herne looked away from the minister and thought again about the pendant, determining that he would have the grave reopened so that the necklace could be laid where it properly belonged.

'Mister Herne. I take offence at your repeated suggestion that I pretended illness for some wicked reason. You have no proof at all of that.'

'No proof?'

'No. It is a most outrageous calumny and I feel that you owe me an apology.'

'I owe you something, that's for certain, and maybe I'll pay you.'

'What is that supposed to mean?'

'If I did have any proof about what I think you did, then I tell you straight *Mister* Minister, that I would have crucified you to the wall of your damned church.'

Turning on his heel Herne stalked back to his horse and rode towards Tucson, ready for the next stage of his mission.

Chapter Eight

Jollye was standing in the main street waiting for him, wringing his hands nervously.

'All went well?'

'Sure.'

'Then you'll be away in the morning?'

'Mister Jollye. I have never found it sound practice to discuss my business while standing in the middle of the road.'

'But you are going?'

'Of course I'm damned well going. Now don't ride my tail and get the money ready to pay into the bank straightaway. I'll be gone from here well before first light and I want the two thousand dollars to my account before then.'

'It'll be there, Mister Herne.'

'It better be.'

By the time that the sun shrank from sight over the hills away to the west, there was a flurry of snow, dusting across the frame houses. Jed put his new horse – a stallion called Jubal – away in the livery stables and walked back past the Mitchell eating-house, towards his own rooms. He had the ammunition he needed for the Colt and for the Sharps, as well as two canteens of water and enough food to keep him going for several days.

Now all he needed was plenty of sleep.

Tucson was quiet, and Herne wondered if he had totally misjudged the priest. Maybe he had been ill. Maybe there wouldn't be any kind of attack. Not on the trail. Not anywhere.

'Jedediah Herne!'

The voice came from the shadows away to his left. His hand fell automatically to the butt of his Colt, flipping off the restraining thong.

'Herne!'

'Who's that?'

With the buildings all around, it was hard to judge whose voice it might be, or precisely where it was coming from.

'Me.'

'Who?'

'Scott Mitchell. Over here by the side door.'

Something was going on. Herne could feel it in his bones. Even allowing for the distortion, there was something wrong with the old man's voice. Some kind of strain.

'What do you want?'

Herne kept his hand on the gun, ready to power himself into immediate action as soon as he could establish what the threat was.

'I want you to . . . to come on over here.' A pause. Then something that sounded like a gasp. Then: 'Come on. I got something to tell you.'

'I hear you.'

There were deep pools of shadow all along the high street, darkened by the heavy clouds, and Herne very slowly and casually eased himself into one of them.

'It's about the train gang.'

'I know everything about them.'

'Cal Ryder is out to get you.'

'That so?' Herne hadn't even known the gang leader's second name, so the old man couldn't possibly have known it.

So?

Scotty Mitchell was being forced to betray him. To try and lure him closer so that someone could gun him down.

It wouldn't be hard to break and run. But there were two objections to that plan.

One was that it would mean Scotty would definitely get shot.

More importantly it could mean that all four members of the gang were in Tucson and Herne might just run right into one of them.

The only way to try and get out of the trap was to go and stick his neck in it.

'I'm comin', Scotty.'

'Jed. Look . . .'

The words were cut off like a razor had been drawn across the old man's throat. Which was possible. Jed had noticed that the Mexican, Diego, had been wearing something in a leather pouch at the back of his neck. It could be a trick that he had picked up from Josiah Hedges, the legendary 'Edge', who had always worn a cut-throat razor in that way.

Still playing innocent, Herne took a few faltering steps towards the side alley, calling out as he did.

'Scotty? You all right in there, Scotty? Damn it, where are you?'

Herne's mind was racing like a train barrelling across the prairies, trying to think how in Hell he could get the bandits out of the alley. He had to get them to start their play first, so that he could know just where they were.

But how?

'Scotty?'

Silence.

The street was deserted, and he wondered just how many people in Tucson had been bought or frightened. The Sheriff hadn't impressed him much. Used to be a fat lawman in Tucson, called Nolan, way back. Old Nolan wouldn't have known what a bribe was and the only thing that frightened him was his beautiful young wife, Heidi.

But he was long dead. Ten years or more.

Nothing lasted, thought Jed bitterly.

'Scotty? You had one of your turns again?'

Maybe the noise of someone nervously shifting a boot in the gritty dirt of the alley.

'Wait on there, old-timer,' he called, the Colt now ready and cocked in his right hand. 'I'll go and get some folks to help. Maybe the Doc to take a look at you.'

He half-turned away, balancing like a great cat, ready to make his move at the first sign.

'Waste him!' yelped a voice from the blackness, and Herne dived to his left, snapping off a couple of shots into the alley.

A volley of shooting came whining back at him, the bullets digging sand up all around him. But the light was poor and he was a moving target.

'Jesus!' Herne screamed, rolling over and over, holding his stomach as though he'd been gut-hit, making sure that he ended up in the cover of a horse-trough, in case they had a long gun with them and just pumped a few slugs into him to make sure he wasn't faking.

'Wait!' called someone. The Mex he thought.

'I got him,' shouted another voice. Danny? Not Cal. Didn't sound like Luke Barrell, and old Luke would have been too cunning to fall for such a simple trick.

It was often the simple ones that worked best. He guessed that the killers must have been waiting up in the alley for some time, their nerves getting stretched like a rustler's neck, waiting for him.

Now he was there, and one of them was confident that he'd shot Herne the Hunter.

Lots of men had thought that over the last twenty or more years. One or two of them had even managed it.

Not this time.

'I'll finish him, Diego!'

It was Danny.

That must mean that there were only the two of them. Cal and Luke choosing to wait up in the safety of the hills to see whether they needed to run or wait. Which meant that Herne had to kill both of them to stop word getting back.

He kept moaning, the pistol ready in his fist, eyes squinting into the dim light across the street to try and make out the figure of the bandit.

There!

Coming in a slanting run, like a huge crab, sidling out of the alley, snapping off a couple of shots as he did, one bullet ripping splinters of wood from the trough within a foot of Herne's head.

If it was Danny, then he wasn't bad. Not that it made any difference to Herne. He'd known shootists who'd claimed they liked to come against top men as they felt better about it.

Herne didn't give a damn. A kid of ten with a scatter-gun would make you just as dead as Wes Hardin with a lightning cross-draw. If they weren't for you, then they had to be against you.

If they were against you, then they were better off dead. That was the simple way of looking at things. The only way if you wanted to stay breathing.

'Danny! It might be a trick!'

'Damn right, Mex,' said Herne softly, steadying the pistol by holding his right wrist with his left hand, sighting at the advancing man. Squeezing the thin trigger once. Feeling the jar run up his wrist, his nostrils filling with the familiar tang of the black powder smoke.

The body of the bandit jerked to a stop as if it had just run into a brick wall, the hands flying out like they were about to embrace an invisible friend. Gun dropping to the earth with a thud.

'Danny!!' screamed Diego from the alley.

The killer sank to his knees, a moan of pain and shock clearly audible to Herne, who was some twenty paces away from him. Clutching his chest where the heavy calibre bullet had hit him. Swaying with the wound.

Carefully, aiming at where the sagging head joined the body, Herne fired once more.

Like a kick in the face it toppled Danny backwards into the dust of the Tucson street. His legs scrabbled for a few seconds, then he lay still.

Lights were coming on all around and a few doors were opening. But still nobody appeared.

As he lay by the trough, Herne quickly replaced the four bullets that he had fired. Trying to put himself into the mind of the Mexican. Trapped in the alley. Having seen his comrade gunned down. Wondering in his turn what Jed was going to do.

'Hey, Senor!'

'What is it, Mex?'

'This old man will be plenty dead in some time soon if you no throw down the gun and let me go.'

'He's nothin' to me, Mex. I kill you whether you kill him or not. I don't care.'

Diego considered this, wondering whether it was true or not.

'I cut him pretty bad, first.'

'I'll take your knee-caps off Mex, and make you crawl from here to Hell and back.'

'Senor!' There was a pleading note in the man's voice, instantly putting Herne on the alert.

'What?'

'I tell you where the others are if you will let me go.'

'If you mean the deserted silver mine up the north trail into the Pinalenos, then save your breath for prayin'.'

A laugh. 'Hey, you know pretty damned lot, Senor. I guess you think you a winner?'

'No winners, Mex. Just a lot of losers.'

Gradually, crawling slowly, Herne began to edge his way towards the alley. When there was the smashing of glass from the darkness.

'He's in the window, Mister,' called out a voice from a half-open doorway.

Herne had guessed that, trying to recall what he could of the inside of the eating-house. Wondering if the Mexican would go on out the back, or try and fool him by coming straight out the front.

From what he knew of Mexican bandits, they were often low on courage, and very high on cunning.

'The front,' he said to himself, standing up, gun ready.

He was right.

The main door exploded as if someone had set off a charge of dynamite inside it, and Diego came charging out, a pistol in each hand spitting fire into the night.

The attack was so violent that Herne was taken partly by surprise, and dived backwards for cover, landing on his shoulder on the edge of the walkway with a jolt that knocked the gun spinning from his hand.

There was enough light from the open doors and windows for Diego to see what had happened and he laughed in delight, standing still in the centre of the street, both guns steady on the helpless man.

'I think maybe you the loser, Senor.'

Herne's eyes were caught by a movement in the darkness of the alley. It was Scotty Mitchell, moving slowly and painfully, tucking a gleaming Colt into the greased holster on his hip. Steadying himself against the corner of the building, wiping a thread of blood from his forehead where they must have pistol-whipped him.

'Come on old-timer,' breathed Jed, trying not to give Mitchell's position away to the Mexican.

'Now the game she is over, Senor. Adios.'

Before he could pull the triggers, there was a shout from behind him. From Scotty.

'Call it, Mex!'

'Dios!' spat Diego, spinning round to face the new threat. Both guns barking in his fists.

There was enough light for Herne to clearly see the puffs of dust spurt from the old man's chest and leg where at least two of the bullets had hit home. Knocking him back against the wall, that held him upright, facing the bandit, his own gun still undrawn.

'You bastard,' said Scotty, his voice slow and heavy with the pain.

Herne started to move for his own gun, then stopped, fascinated by the grim tableau being played out across the street from him.

Diego was standing still, unable to believe that the old man was still upright with the bullets in him. Not firing again. Just waiting.

'Greasy son of a bitch!' said Scotty, his voice louder. Hand feeling for the gun on his hip. Body slanting in a bizarre parody of a gunfighter's fast draw. Like watching it done in a dream. Slowed down like someone fighting underwater.

The hand coming up from the holster, with the gun in it. Scotty tried to cock it with one hand but the effect was too great for him and he brought the left hand across to help himself.

Although Herne was conscious of people all around watching, from doors and windows, there was no sound. Just the lone wind bringing the taste of snow in it. And the click of the pistol as the hammer was drawn back.

'No,' called the Mexican, snapping off another flurry of shots. At least two of them hit home, making Mitchell stagger. It wasn't possible that he could still stand there.

But he did.

Bringing up the Colt as if it was a religious relic of infinite value, cradling it in both hands, holding it out in front of his chest, aiming it with great care at the Mexican.

Diego couldn't believe it, and he looked round at Herne, as if he sought reassurance that this nightmare wasn't happening to him. But Jed shrugged, knowing that this hand needed to be played out right to the end, his only other movement being the quick step needed to pick up his own gun.

In case.

The old man's pistol boomed, the flash of the flame nearly obscured by the burst of smoke from the muzzle.

Jed was a few paces behind the Mexican, and it seemed to him as if the man's head had burst. The bullet hit him in the temple, angling off and distorting as it ploughed through the skull and ripped the brain apart. Knocking the sombrero off Diego's head.

The bandit danced back a few steps under the impact, as if he was fighting for his balance, but it was only a reflex action from the dying brain. The strings were cut and Diego's body slumped untidily in the middle of the Tucson street, and lay motionless.

Herne jumped over him, knowing that there was no need to bother further about him, sprinting to where Scotty Mitchell leaned against the wall of the eating-house. The gun had fallen from his fingers, and he was slowly sliding down the side of the building.

'Gramps!' screamed a girl's voice in the crowd. Jed turned to see Ellie-May running towards him, skirts flying. He caught her in his arms and stopped her going to the old man.

'No.'

'But he . . .'

'No, Ellie-May. Scotty's done what he had to do. Wait here.'

The side of the wall was splintered where the Mexican's bullets had passed clean through the frail body of the old gunfighter, and blood smeared all the way down to where Mitchell half sat, half lay, looking up at Herne.

'Sorry 'bout the trap, Jed, but . . .'

'It doesn't signify, Scotty.'

There was a kind of a smile from the dying man. He didn't seem to be in any pain, but Jed had seen the bullets hit him and knew that life was a matter of seconds for him.

'I get him?'

'Course.'

'Dead?'

'As a fish in ice.'

'That's mighty good.'

'You saved my life, old timer,' said Herne, putting away his own gun.

'Said I'd come a'runnin', didn't I?'

'You sure did.'

It was a scene that Herne had lived through more times than he could remember. Having a friend die right in front of you and nothing to be done. Though he'd only known Scotty Mitchell a couple days, he'd been a shootist, like Herne. And he'd done what he could in a tight corner. That made him a friend.

'Guess this is the end of the trail, Jed.'

'I wouldn't lie to you. You should have stayed safe in the alley.'

The head shook. 'Nope. Man couldn't ask a better way to ... to go. Savin' a life. Wastin' a no-good. Smell of the powder smoke. I ain't sad 'bout it.'

Herne stood silent and watched the life ebbing. Hearing the girl crying behind him, and the muttering from the crowd in the street.

Scott Mitchell peered up at Herne through eyes that were misting over. 'You ... know something? I saw George Custer when he ...'

The voice faded away like the dew on morning grass and the old man was dead. Herne walked back to his room through the cold of the evening.

Chapter Nine

Herne left instructions with Jollye that some of the money was to be given to Ellie-May Mitchell to pay for the funeral of the old man.

He slept well, rising early to get ready for the journey up into the Mountains. He had told the owner of the livery stable that he wanted Jubal watered and saddled for a start before dawn, and the man had done what he asked. The bay stallion was brushed down and tethered in his stall when Jed arrived, giving him a whinny of recognition.

The wind had dropped, but the town was dusted with another fall of snow. Just enough to bear the hoof-marks as Herne walked the horse along the deserted main street of Tucson, passing the place where Scott Mitchell had died. The broken door had been boarded up, and there was a solitary light gleaming yellow in an upstairs window.

It took Jed Herne a long, hard day's riding to get near the point where the trail vanished off north towards the towering peaks of the Pinalenos. Heeling Jubal along through the massive saguaro cactuses, the horse's hooves raising a cloud of red-orange dust.

This was Apache country. Mescaleroes.

There hadn't been a lot of trouble in that territory for some time, but that didn't mean that it would stay that way. Salt River Canyon and Turret Butte were only ten years back, and the dances and the rituals were still performed in the lonely fastnesses among the silent mountains of the Southwest.

Jed prepared his camp with great care, choosing a spot overlooking a dry stream-bed, high enough up to be safe in case of a winter flash-flood. He would have appreciated a fire to keep out the biting cold, but he was only a few miles from the old mining-camp of Norwich Hills, and in the clear light a red glow would be seen for a long, long way.

He wrapped himself in a pair of blankets, huddling down against the freezing wind, hoping the weather wouldn't get any worse. Snow in the high country came fast and stayed long.

Few people appreciated that better than Jedediah Travis Herne. Several times in his life snow had left its mark on him.

It had been indirectly responsible for his birth, and for the death of his mother. Albert Jedediah Herne was a leading map-maker and an associate of the famous explorer, J. C. Frémont. Jed's mother, Elizabeth Julia, was with her husband on the Frémont expedition that was surveying over the high Sierras in the early part of 1844. Although heavy with child, she had believed that they would have been able to return to the safety of civilization well before her time came.

The snow changed all that.

A blizzard had trapped the entire party up in Carson Pass, keeping them there for day after day. The delay meant that the expected child was born far from any of the comforts of home and doctor. The rough campsite was cold and desolate, and the delivery a difficult one.

The last day of February 1844, a leap year, saw the birth day of Jed Herne. A squalling, sturdy child, he survived until the snow cleared and they could all come down in safety.

All except his mother, Elizabeth Herne, whose bones would lie for ever in that barren wilderness.

Christened Jedediah after his father, and Travis after the defender of the Alamo, the baby was immediately given into the care of his father's unmarried sister, Rosemary, who had lived in Boston.

The shock of his wife's death disturbed Albert Herne, and he never saw the child again, vanishing in Indian country while on a solitary expedition in the Fall of that same year of 1844.

The gentle, weak, and mildly alcoholic old lady in Boston was no match for the wild young Jed and he ran away from home several times, finding both bad company and the wrong side of the law.

At the age of fifteen Jed Herne killed his first man.

To escape retribution from the dead man's friends, he headed west, finding that the Pony Express was just setting up in business on the dangerous run from Fort Bridger westwards and was seeking young riders.

It was the perfect job and by the time he was sixteen Jed Herne was one of their top men. The winter of 1860 was a bitter one. The Paiutes had risen but the Pony Express must get through.

Sitting shivering in the windy darkness of the Pinaleno foothills, Herne chewed on a piece of jerky and thought back to those days.

Back to the spunky young boy, a year younger than Jed, who had ridden with him. Travelling together on one occasion better than three hundred and fifty miles with no sleep. The boy's name had been Bill Cody.

Last Jed heard of Bill Cody he'd been making a name massacring huge numbers of buffalo for the railroad companies.

Jed remembered those days. The pain, with the mind

forcing the exhausted body on. There had been snow then. Deep drifts over the Sierras that had risen to the bellies of their horses.

The memories of the past vanished as he heard a noise out in the brush. A light sound, that might have been the wind rolling a dry twig along over the rocks. Or might have been the scuffling of a soft leather boot.

The moon was a thin sliver of silver lurking behind driven clouds, giving barely enough light to see the dim shape of Jubal standing patiently on the far side of the small clearing.

One man travelling alone would stand out to the eyes of the Apaches like a rat in a bowl of flour. Since it was unlikely that a white man carrying anything worthwhile would be travelling alone then it was also unlikely that the local Mescalero would bother to attack him.

But you never knew with the Indians. Especially Apaches.

Taking no chances, Jed drew the Colt and rolled out of the folds of the blankets, crouching, trying to see who or what was close.

Mountain lion? Maybe even a bear.

Still the best bet was that it was a man.

Moving in slow, silent steps, Jed crept to the edge of the clearing away from the stallion. That way he wouldn't disturb Jubal and give away his own position. And he was ready for anyone coming in that side.

As he waited, he strained his ears. Suddenly aware that the hillside around him was alive with men. Maybe as many as twenty. Although the white man feared the strange cunning of Indians, claiming that they could ghost through stone walls and out again, Herne knew that they were simply skilled craftsmen in tracking and hunting. But that didn't make them perfect. An Apache could no more move in total silence over dry grass and sticks than a white man could.

The Mescaleroes were closing in. There was no doubt

about it. Against that many, Herne knew that he had two chances: very slim and none at all.

Why so many should be out just after him was a puzzle. The first time he caught the sound he wondered if it was either Cal Ryder or Luke Barrell hedging their bets by watching the trail.

There was the faint cry of a wild bird. Echoing around him. Mournful in the vast cold space of the mountains. A cry that was repeated from both sides of the clearing. A third time from very close to him. They must be within a few dozen paces of him, circling steadily in.

He peered out to where his blankets still lay, hoping that they resembled a sleeping man. If they made a final charge, then his slim chance would be that they might pass him by in the blackness and give him a hope of heading for higher ground.

In his travels, Jed had picked up a little of the Indian's language. Enough to get by in the basics with either Plains Indians or the smaller men from the mountains. With so many Apaches around him, calling their signals to each other, there was a chance that there might be talking, and he could then know what was happening.

He flattened himself to the ground, oblivious now to the cold and the wind. All of his senses concentrating on the job of survival. Shielding the weapon under his coat to muffle the sound, Herne cocked the pistol, holding it in his right hand. Considering whether to draw the knife from his boot, and deciding that it was better on balance to leave it where it was as a last resort.

Another spate of bird cries.

Closer.

There was a towering cactus behind him, its stark prickly limbs crucified black against the faint light of the sky. All around was low brush and spear-grass. Giving good cover among the stunted trees, but leaving dry leaves beneath, so that total silence wasn't possible.

Absolutely still, Herne lay and waited.

Only a couple of yards away, there was the harsh whisper of two men talking. One ordering the other to a course of action. Herne couldn't make it all out.

There was another splutter of chatter. It seemed to be an older man telling a much younger one to go in and kill. That much was clear. It seemed almost to be some sort of a test.

If it was a warrior being prepared in such a way, then it would make sense of attacking a lone white man. And other braves would have come along as well to witness how the young warrior bore himself.

Herne tried desperately to see where the nearest of the Apaches was, wondering if it might be as well to try a break now while they weren't prepared. Then he heard something that gave him a glimmer of an idea.

'Go and kill as son of chief should,' was the nearest he could get in translation.

So. It was the son of a local tribal chief, being blooded in front of all the warriors. With Herne as his target.

Jed slid forwards into a crouch, the gun still gripped in his fist. Listening for the sound of the attacker coming in towards him.

Hearing the faint scrape of the leather boots, and then the whisper of strained breathing. To have to kill an enemy in the darkness like this, even a man you thought was sleeping, would put great pressure on a boy, and his nerves would be stretched to breaking point.

There!

The silhouette of a slim figure, against the sky, stepping with feet raised high, putting them down each time with exaggerated care. Walking past the crouching man close enough to touch, unaware that the white man was even there.

All around was silence. Herne was conscious of the remainder of the Apaches waiting, hoping for success, ready to move in case of trouble. The wind had eased, but the clouds were building up, promising worse weather to come soon.

The boy was past him, focusing all his attention on the dark shadow of the blankets. Herne caught the gleam of light off the broad-bladed knife in his right hand. Held point downwards ready for the stabbing thrust to the heart.

Keeping low, so that none of the other Indians would see him, Jed began to creep in behind the young warrior, easing the hammer forwards silently so that the pin rested on the cartridge. Making sure that his grip on the butt was firm and safe.

Jubal whinnied suddenly, and skittered sideways, possibly scenting the Apaches all around him in the brush. Covered by the noise, Herne closed right in behind the Mescalero boy.

Who had checked his advance at the horse's movement, pausing on the edge of the clearing, bracing himself for the final charge.

Herne judged the moment to perfection, raising the heavy pistol and bringing it down in a solid arc, hitting the young man at the base of the skull. The crunching blow was softened a little by the mane of black hair that tumbled to his shoulders, but it was still hard enough to knock him instantly unconscious.

As the body slumped forwards, Jed caught it under the arms, holding it upright, pressing the muzzle of the Colt to the boy's head, supporting him with the left hand. The knife dropped with a light tinkle to the stones, and Herne tensed himself ready for the next few seconds.

They would determine whether he lived or died.

From behind him in the darkness came a whisper. Asking the young man what had happened.

Racking his brain for the right words, Herne replied in a loud clear voice.

'Keep men quiet or boy dies. I have him with gun.'

There was an instant babble of voices from all around him, drowned out by a loud shout for silence from the man that Jed guessed was the chief. The father of the young boy he held at gun-point.

'You speak Apache tongue?'

'Not well. Do you speak English?'

A pause. 'Some. You are clever white man.'

'Clever enough not to send a boy on a job for a man.'

'He lives?'

'He lives. Do you want him to go on living?'

'Yes. What is the price?'

Herne hesitated. Despite the white man's mistrust of the honesty of some Indians, he knew enough of the code of honour of the Apaches to be prepared to take a gamble on trusting them. Not that there was an awful lot of choice for him.

'Who are you?'

'I am what you call Man Runs On Air. I am chief of Mescalero tribe of Apache nation.'

Herne knew the name. Man Runs On Air had won his name when he and three other braves had been captured several years back on one side of a knife-edge canyon. The cavalry had them surrounded and called on the four Apaches to surrender.

Although there was a great yawning chasm between them and safety, the Indians chose to try and leap it. Three of the four fell screaming to a mangling death. Only one man survived the jump. Man Runs On Air.

'I am Jedediah Herne, called Herne the Hunter.'

Though he rarely used his nickname, he knew that it might help to impress the Apaches.

'I know of you. You have taken prisoner of my son. He was to kill you as test for warrior.'

'I can kill him.'

'Yes. Then we kill you, and you will not die quick.'

'I know that also. If I spare his life, then you will also let me go freely on my way? You will not try and have me followed?'

'I must talk with others. Wait and do not harm boy. Can he speak?'

'I laid him out cold with the butt of my pistol, but he's still breathing well. Don't take too long over the talking, chief.'

The boy was showing signs of recovering consciousness, beginning to struggle feebly. Herne tightened the grip around his throat, pressing the barrel of the Colt hard into the side of his head.

'Don't move, boy. Just stay quiet and easy and maybe we both go on living.'

Despite the chill of the night, Jed was sweating, feeling droplets running down the small of his back, soaking through his shirt. He kept moving around, changing the direction, in case Man Runs On Air decided to send in a warrior to try and beat the finger on the trigger with a snap shot. In the darkness it wasn't likely, but it wasn't a risk worth the taking.

There was the sound of movement in the brush around the clearing and Herne called out again. 'Anyone comes any nearer and your son loses his head, chief.'

'We have spoken. My son has been wrong to be trapped by you. But we know of Herne the Hunter and he must not pay too much price for foolishness. If you release him then you go free.'

'Not just for tonight, Man Runs On Air. Your word that no warrior of your people will harm me while I remain in these mountains.'

'Wait.'

The boy made an attempt to wriggle free and knee Herne in the groin. With no effort at all Jed half-turned, bracing his hip into the lad's back, croaking the elbow into his windpipe and nearly strangling him. There was a gurgling moan and then he went limp in Herne's arms.

'What was that, Herne the Hunter?'

'The cub tried to bite.'

There was a note of anxiety in the voice of the Mescalero leader. 'You have harmed him?'

'He sleeps.'

'What?' There was a depth of anger in the cry that made Herne tighten his finger on the trigger.

'He sleeps and soon he will wake. But he fights me and it is hard not to hurt him. I would have your word of my safety here.'

'How many days do you stay?'

'I seek two men who are thieves.'

'Apache?'

'White men.'

Suddenly there was an easing of the tension.

'One in the clothes of a God-man? The other tall and in black? Three horses?'

'Could be.'

'They are in old mine.'

'Norwich Hills?'

'Yes.'

'Guessed so, but I'm still obliged to you for that. They still there?'

There was a quick exchange between the unseen chief and one of his warriors.

'Yes. They are there. There was two men also. They have gone two days back. They also bad men?'

'Not any more. I killed them yesterday. So I am free to go?'

'For . . . five days. After that I cannot give my word. You know what young men are?'

Herne grinned at the resignation in the voice of Man Runs On Air.

'Yes. I know. Five days will be fine. Should let me do what I need. Thanks.'

'My son?'

'Just waking up again. You want me to leave him here, or will you come in and get him?'

There was no hesitation this time. 'He is my son, Herne the Hunter. I will come and get him. Stand there.'

Someone called out from the blackness, and Man Runs On Air replied angrily. Herne guessed that it had been a warning of possible treachery.

There was a darkening of the night at his elbow, and he smelled the oil on the skin of the chief. The two older men stood together in silence, until Herne released the boy, steadying him when he nearly fell. Feeling as exposed as he ever had in his life, Jed holstered the Colt, and stood there, aware of the cold again.

Man Runs On Air said something to the young man who slunk away into the blackness of the hillside. Then the chief called out to the rest of his warriors, who responded to the shout.

'You are safe, Herne the Hunter. May you hunt well.'

'I thank you. It has been good to know such a great warrior, Man Runs On Air.'

There was the briefest clasp of hands and then the Apache vanished into the chill night, taking his men with him.

In a couple of minutes the clearing and the brush around

it were as empty as if the incident had never happened. Jed squinted at his watch, reading the time with difficulty. From beginning to end it could not have taken more than twenty minutes.

Five minutes later he was asleep again.

Chapter Ten

Snow threatened.

When Jed woke, cold seeping into the marrow of his bones, the first light of the morning hardly scraped at the surface of the night. Cloud wrapped the land in a dull grey shroud, and the wind was rising again. Blowing the dust into small pillars of red sand that collapsed in on themselves.

He sipped a couple of mouthfuls of water from one of the canteens, and ate some more of the jerky. Jed was so chilled that he had to run around and do vigorous exercises to get the blood flowing again. Clapping his hands together, feeling the tips of his fingers tingling. He glanced around, seeing the mist that enveloped the tips of the Pinalenos, his brow wrinkling as he wondered how long it would be before the snow came.

Norwich Hills had sprung up, flourished and died all within a couple of years. A chase after a double killer had taken Jedediah Herne there some years back, and he could still remember the place. Already fading when he got there. He'd gunned down the man he wanted on the porch of what used to be the church.

He'd heard that the mine had closed and the little township had gone back to the wilderness of cactus and stone that had been there long before. Now it was a ghost town, a few miles into the hills on a winding road barely wide enough for a wagon.

As he pushed Jubal forwards through the dust and sleet

that the wind was carrying, Jed stared down at the rutted trail. Seeing where the rain had washed out sections of the trail so that it was no wider than four or five feet.

At one turn of the track a slide had completely blocked it off, and he saw there were the prints of five horses going in. Two coming out. That meant that Cal and Luke were still in the place. Holed up and waiting for Danny and the Mexican to come back and tell them it was safe to move.

Only they weren't coming back.

Not ever.

Because of the formation of the Pinaleno range at that point, Herne knew that there was no practical way out of Norwich Hills. A man alone, carrying a few days' supply of water, might make it.

Might make it.

But the trail stopped dead at the far end of the one street through Norwich Hills. Just past where there used to be a blacksmith. Beyond that there was raw stone and jagged ridges. Rising and falling until you got across forty or fifty miles of nothingness to the main western trail towards Phoenix. And by the time you got to Phoenix you'd be near to dying.

One trail into the mining camp.

The same trail out again.

There was a battered notice-board at a turn of the trail, not far from where Jed remembered the township began.

It lay on its side in the dust, half-covered. He swung down from the saddle, stretching his legs, feeling the strain of the long ride. Walked over to the board and pulled it out.

Someone had been using it for target practice, but all of the bullet-holes were years old. The wood weathered and torn.

The paint had faded over the years, but it was still readable.

'Welcome to Norwich Hills. Fastest growing little town in the Arizona Territory.'

Then it said that the population was one hundred and eighty-seven souls. At least, that seemed to be the highest number in a line of altered figures. Some crossed through. Some left.

As the population of the township rose with the lure of the silver, so it fell again when the lode ran out. And the numbers decreased. Down and down.

Herne stooped and peered at the board, trying to read what was written in white paint, the letters uneven and sprawling.

'I hav berried the last. It is ovr.' There was a signature, but it was illegible.

Whoever he'd been, he'd been right. But now the little ghost town was enjoying a flourishing revival. At present the population stood at two, with Herne about to make it three.

But if all went well it wouldn't be long before Norwich Hills was down to one again.

Then to nobody.

Jed had remounted Jubal and walked him along until he reached the point in the trail where he knew he would be able to see down a small dip towards Norwich Hills. Along the trail, straight at that point, to the collection of ramshackle buildings, with the old mine working perched above it.

Not wanting to trot into view of anyone watching, he dismounted again and tethered the bay stallion to a large boulder, in the lee of the biting wind. Howling in among the mountains all about, it was carrying a few flakes of snow on it. Whisking them about, blowing them into Herne's face so that he could taste them cold and sharp on his tongue.

Shading his eyes against the swirling snow, Herne stalked forward, the Sharps rifle gripped in one hand, shrugging his shoulders, sinking his head lower into the collar of his coat.

There was a ridge, and he moved slowly towards it, warily creeping through a jumble of scattered rocks until he could see down into what remained of the township.

'Jesus,' he whispered to himself as he saw what several years had done to Norwich Hills.

His memory had been of a typical small township, centred around a narrow street, with the houses and saloons and brothel jostling each other on a steep hill. And above it all hung the mine, gaunt wooden piling scattered all around it.

That was how it had been.

Now there was virtually nothing left. It looked as if there had been a massive land-slip, obliterating all but a couple of the buildings. The street had gone, but Jed could make out a few tracks over the pile of red dirt, heading up towards the mine.

There again nature had been at work. Ripping down the skeletal derricks and winding-gear, leaving only two or three small huts around the base of the diggings, with another close by the gaping tunnel of the main shaft into the mountain.

That was all.

Sheer beyond it rose the Pinalenos Mountains, their tops obscured by driving snow and cloud. When Herne had been there before it had been in baking heat, the orange dust blowing everywhere.

There was Norwich Hills.

Where were Cal Ryder and Luke Barrell?

The blizzard was worsening so fast that there was no danger of his being seen, but there was a risk that his horse might die. A quarter of the distance to the shattered remnants of Norwich Hills there was the shell of a building, with a corner of the roof still hanging on to the beams.

If it hadn't been for the storm, he would never have dared risk bringing Jubal along that trail, but visibility had closed down to only fifty yards or so. Even if Cal and Luke were there, and Herne didn't doubt they were, there was no risk of them seeing or hearing the stallion.

Slithering around on the carpet of freezing snow, Herne returned and brought the horse along to the old shed, leading it into the comparative warmth and safety of the building. Despite the huge holes in the roof, there was shelter remaining to keep Jubal from freezing to death or becoming buried in the snow.

Herne tethered him to a fallen rafter, throwing one of his own blankets over his back, patting him on the flank before walking out again into the teeth of the blizzard.

If the Apaches said that the white men hadn't been seen leaving Norwich Hills, then that meant they hadn't left it. Since the main street was so flattened and destroyed, the odds seemed to be that they would be up nearer the mine, where the handful of huts would offer the best chance of protection.

Carrying the Sharps, Herne clambered down towards the street, constantly stopping to wipe snow from his face and eyes. Nerves alert for any sign of either of the men. In that sort of situation, he might easily walk straight into them, unable as he was to see more than a few yards. Then it would be down to who was quicker. Herne knew that he'd have the edge, because he knew that they were there. They had no idea where he was, but they must have had a reasonable hope that he would be lying dead in a Tucson alley by now.

For a few moments the snow eased, just as he came level with the first of the remaining houses in the street. Aware that the lull would expose him to anyone looking out, Herne dodged into the building, feeling the floor-boards creaking under his boot-heels.

The interior had been stripped at some time when the township was dying, and little remained to show what it had been. Jed couldn't remember who might once have owned it, but guessed it had been a private dwelling.

An old mattress lay crumpled in one corner of the floor, with stains on it that showed it had been through a variety of uses. A large black mark in the centre was long-dried blood.

On the wall immediately above it, someone had used a stub of blunt pencil to write the words: 'It was God that made me a prostitute.'

In another hand beneath it someone had scrawled: 'If I give him five dollars will he make one for me?'

The dust was so thick inside the wrecked house that it was obvious that nobody had set foot in it for several months. More probably for several years.

So Jed felt safe enough in using it as a temporary base. He clambered up the rickety remains of the stairs to look out through the snow towards the huts clustered about the mouth of the Norwich Hills mine.

It was only a little after midday, but the light was poor, and he squinted through the cracked window-pane to see if he could detect any sign of life.

A spider's web fluttered at the edge of the glass, trembling in the draught. Across the land-slip and up the hill, Herne saw that the snow was banking up. From what he remembered the main shaft ran into the side of the hill, with another deep pit opening up a hundred yards or so away, where they'd been trying to find another way of reaching the mother lode.

The group of huts was just visible, and he watched in silence for several minutes, the first nagging doubts beginning to creep into his mind.

Suppose they weren't there?

In a lull in the storm he saw a black square appear in the side of one of the huts. A door was being opened. A figure appeared and looked out at the blizzard. Then the door was quickly shut again.

Herne let out a sigh of contentment.

They were there.

Chapter Eleven

The range was about six hundred yards.

On the flat, with reasonable weather and visibility, Herne would have risked a shot at the bandit. If you got hit by the great, booming, fifty-five calibre bullet of the Sharps rifle, then most times you stayed hit.

But this wasn't a shot worth making.

There was no good rest for the long rifle. It was uphill. Through snow and poor light. With a gusty wind that veered from light breeze to screeching gale from moment to moment.

Herne was faced with a difficult choice.

If he stayed where he was in the relative comfort of the make-shift shelter, the storm might go on for days before it blew itself out. Water would be no problem, and he could probably have lasted on the small amount of dried meat he had with him. There had been times when he had survived as long as nine days without proper food.

But it was the cold that would kill him if he waited there. With no food to stoke the boilers of his body, it would eat at him. He had seen it other times with other men. The way that even strong fighting shootists would give up. Sit down and refuse to get up again. Gradually slipping into a strange sort of waking sleep. The blood flowing slower round their bodies. Until they finally closed their eyes and never got round to opening them again.

Also, if he waited where he was, they might realize that

Diego and Danny weren't coming back. They'd take fright and move out. Possibly at night when he was sleeping. If he missed them then he lost all chance of retrieving the pendant. As well as giving up on three thousand dollars for the printing plates.

It was damned difficult.

Because the other alternative left to him was to go in after them. Get closer and hope to pick one, or both, of them off. But they might not come out. Herne wasn't about to bust in the door with his foot and rush in shooting. He'd seen the pulp magazines that portrayed heroes who did that sort of thing. All it would get him would be a bellyful of lead.

To spend more than a couple of hours outside in the wind and snow would also be enough to kill him off.

It was damned difficult.

Cal and Luke would be expecting their two comrades back in Norwich Hills by nightfall. Allowing for the weather, they might not begin to worry much until the next morning.

So Herne had, at least, that much time.

Until dawn there wasn't much that he could do. If the weather changed appreciably during the next fifteen hours or so, it would wake him.

So he slept.

Easily and dreamlessly.

There had been nights when he had woken sweating with the horrors of his wife's death rising before him in a dream. It had been like that after the living nightmare of Lawrence, when he had ridden with Quantrill and his Raiders and they'd butchered and slaughtered and burned. He'd been very young then. Apart from the notorious gang of Northern butchers, led by Caleb Thorn, Quantrill's men had been the worst.

Not many men could sleep easy after seeing what the young Jedediah Herne had seen.

Several times an alteration in the force or the direction of the wind disturbed him, and he would roll out of his one blanket, glancing through the dusty window at the leaden sky.

Each time it was only a minor change, and each time he slipped back into sleep. It had been Doc Holliday who had told him, between coughing blood into an embroidered lace 'kerchief, that the human body stored sleep, and that it was always a good idea to catch up on it whenever the chance came. It seemed a sensible idea and Jed had always tried to follow it.

Not that there were a whole mess of chances for long sleeping when you were a hired gun or a bounty hunter. Sleep too long and you might never wake up.

First light brought him to his feet, slipping the Colt back into its holster. All through the night it had remained in his hand. Throwing the blanket over his shoulder like a poncho, walking to the window, feeling the cold stiffening his muscles. Wondering what he was doing, at forty years of age, punishing himself like this.

The thought passed.

The wind was definitely easier. The next building up the street, close to the earth-slip, had a single shutter remaining on one of the first floor windows, and it flapped ceaselessly to and fro. But it wasn't battering itself to splinters the way it had been the night before.

The whole of Norwich Hills was shrouded in snow, the whiteness blurring the outlines of the mining equipment, leaving the black mouth of the shaft gaping more clearly, like a bullet hole in white skin.

There was a thread of grey smoke drifting away from the hut where Herne had seen the figure appear. Its door stood partly open. Even as Herne watched through the clear light of the morning, he saw one of the two men – Luke, he thought from the build – come from behind one of the tangled heaps of wood and wire and hurry into the hut. He seemed to be buttoning up his clothes.

With the snow no longer falling, and the wind dropped, Herne might have risked a shot at him, but the Sharps lay on the floor.

He looked at the thickness of the snow hanging on the angled roof of the building next door, judging that close to eighteen inches had fallen during the previous storm. Enough to slow down a man on foot, but not enough to stop a horseman escaping from Norwich Hills.

'Time to be movin',' said Herne to himself, spinning the chamber of the Colt by habit, making sure he carried a full load. If he'd ever stopped to think about it he'd have laughed at it; if anyone filed a half inch off the nose of one bullet in the gun, he'd have known it the moment he drew it, the alteration in the delicate balance of the pistol would have warned him.

But habits died hard.

Once he was out of the door and across the further side of the slip he would be out of sight of the hut. If he went fast he could cut the odds against them moving while he was also unable to see them. In the old days there had been back gullies along the whole length of the street, but the erosion of earth and wind and rain had altered all that, and the rear of the house teetered perilously over a sheer drop to a canyon three or four hundred feet deep.

Snow, banked several feet deep, blocked off the doorway, forcing Herne to clamber over splintered and rotting boards to get out through one of the windows, knocking out a few gleaming shards of glass from the corner of the frame.

Before he moved from the shadow of the building, Jed

eased the thong down over the hammer of the Colt, not prepared to take a chance on it slipping out of the oiled holster if he fell in the snow.

The rifle was in his left hand, half-hidden under the grey blanket. Herne paused a moment, staring up the incline towards the old workings of the Norwich Hills mine, concentrating all his attention on the hut where he'd seen Luke Barrell. Apart from a tell-tale thread of smoke worming from a ramshackle metal chimney, it gave the impression of being deserted. The door was closed and there didn't seem to be any windows. Though there could easily be cracks. Perhaps the two men were actually watching him as he stood there. Maybe both with rifles. Both with a bead on him. Just waiting for the moment to shoot.

If it was a difficult shot aiming up the hill, it would be an impossible one down towards the street. He looked at the snow that drifted across the trail in a sullen, shifting pall of dusty white. Trying to guess if there were any deep ruts concealed by it, where he might turn an ankle or fall and break a leg.

There didn't seem to be anything and he gathered himself like a sprinter at the start of a race, powering from the shade of the stoop and bounding across to the other side, disappearing over the edge of the trail in a flurry of ice and snow.

Panting with the effort, Herne watched his breath pluming away and vanishing as the dying wind caught it. Despite the fact that it was no longer snowing, it was still bitingly cold, and he rubbed his fingers to keep the blood flowing. The art of the shootist was a variable one at the best of times, but in cold weather it became more hazardous. It was so easy to fumble. To miss the first vital grip on the butt. Or the thumb could miss the first pull on the hammer.

Sliding and floundering through snow that sometimes

reached his groin, Herne clambered up the edge of the draw until he could once again see the hut that was his target. As far as he could tell, nothing had altered in the few minutes that he'd been out of sight. The smoke still stood like a wisp of grey flag, and the door was still closed.

It had been grindingly hard physical work, and Jed lay back out of sight, wiping sweat from his head with the corner of the blanket. Checking the guns hadn't been damaged by the deep snow.

Then working his way around higher up, slipping down four yards for every five he climbed. Pausing every now and then to peek over the brim of the draw to check all was unchanged.

Once he thought he heard the whinny of a horse. It seemed to come from the mouth of the mine, but it was hard to tell. It might even have been Herne's own horse, Jubal, registering its protest at being left alone with nothing to eat for the whole night.

It took more than an hour to reach the position that he wanted. High on the flank of the hill, nestled down among snow-packed boulders, with a fine view down on the hut. Less than three hundred yards from the door.

As he looked at the workings of the mine, the main shaft that ran into the mountain was nearly below him; a little to his right. The hut was further away. Then came the tangle of metal and fallen struts where the cables and the buckets had run down into Norwich Hills with the ore.

Circled with rubbish was the mouth of the pit that had been bored, futilely, to try and save the mine from closing when the vein of silver ran out.

He heard the noise of horses once again, and guessed that they must be just inside the old mine working, sheltered from the weather.

There was something else interesting that Herne was now

able to spot from his eyrie. A line of tracks led through the snow to a flimsy wooden screen about six feet high by eight feet wide. It was just possible to glimpse that the snow behind it was pitted and trodden, indicating where Luke and Cal had been going to relieve their bodily needs.

Away to his right there was another cluster of boulders that would bring him within one hundred yards of the screen, and Herne decided to take the chance and move to it. Stepping like a fox on ice across the slippery slope, twice nearly falling. Saving himself by jabbing the barrel of the Sharps hard into the packed snow to hold him like a climber's axe.

If anyone had walked from the hut during that climb, and looked up towards the snow-wrapped peaks of the Pinalenos, they couldn't have failed to see Herne stuck there like a fly pinned to a sheet of white paper. But he made it, sitting resting in his new position, able to look down from a place of authority.

The Sharps was already loaded. He cocked it, licking his finger and holding it up; to be sure of the veering wind. Looking round him to see if and when the sun would break through. There was such heavy cloud cover that it seemed likely more storms were on the way.

'One hundred ... maybe one-twenty,' he said, adjusting the sights on the long gun.

It was an easy shot for a gun like the fifty-five Sharps. Much of the area behind the frail screen was now visible to him.

He rested the barrel of the gun on the rocks and sat and waited.

It was twenty-eight minutes before eight. Even as Herne was tucking the pocket-watch back in an inside pocket of his coat he saw the dark shape of the door opening, on the side of the hut nearest to the remnants of the township.

And out came Luke Barrell.

Still wearing the clothes of the priest, right down to the roman collar. He called something back inside the little square building, and Herne heard the soft voice of Cal Ryder answering him.

He eased the barrel forward among the rocks, pointing it in the general direction of Barrell, waiting until he was clear of the hut before risking a shot. He wasn't totally confident that the bang the Sharps had taken on the rutted ice might not have damaged the foresight.

The door shut again, and Barrell hopped like a scalded frog along the path. Jed noticed that the man was barefooted, so he guessed that what he planned to do behind that leaning wall wasn't likely to take long.

Because of his worry about the sighting of the rifle, Herne decided to take a shot at the planks while the bandit was still out of sight. Aiming at a prominent knot-hole almost dead in the centre.

The notch of the sight lined up as he held his breath, finger caressing the trigger. Like all first-rate shots Jed fired two-eyed, not squinting along the barrel with one eye shut.

The familiar boom of the charge, and the cloud of black powder smoke that virtually obscured the target. Herne waved it aside with his hand, screwing up his forehead when he saw that the shot hadn't hit the mark he had aimed at. It had torn a great hole in the wood a hand's span to the right and an inch or so high. As he reloaded the gun, Jed was mentally refiring the shot with that correction built into it. At the same time aware of the effect the bullet had made.

'Hey!'

There was no reply from inside the hut. It looked as if it had been built strong enough to withstand the effects of blasting and it was quite possible that the man inside wouldn't have heard the noise of the shot.

'Hey! Cal, you brainless son of a bitch! That damned near hit me while I was . . . No!!!'

The second bullet must have been closer. And it went precisely where Jed had aimed. With a Sharps rifle, accuracy at such a short range of a hundred yards went without even saying.

'Cal! Will you . . .?'

Jed levered a fresh round into the breech, quickly sighting and firing a third time. A touch to the right this time.

'Aaaaahh!'

There was a glimpse of a leg flailing about behind the one side of the screen and Jed snapped off a quick fourth shot at it, having the satisfaction of seeing it jerk and hearing another scream of pain.

'Jesus! Cal! You dirty double-crossin' bastard. Come out like a man.'

Luke Barrell must have been wearing his gun, as Herne saw the puffs of smoke from a pistol bursting from behind the wooden wall, and heard the lighter crack of the shots.

Four of them hit the walls of the hut where Cal Ryder was waiting. Maybe even asleep.

'Cal! Now stop it, you hear. I'm hurt bad.'

'Got to get worse before it gets better was what I always heard!' yelled Herne from the safety of the snow-covered rocks.

'Who the . . .? Who the Hell's that?'

'Remember the Bozeman Trail, Luke?'

'What?'

'Near Fort Laramie.'

'Agent?'

'Bounty, Luke. I was there.'

'Jesus. Back in seventy-one?'

'Seventy.'

'Come out and let's see you.'

'Gun-runnin' to Arapaho bucks isn't pretty, Luke, nor is leavin' your friends to dangle in the wind.'

'*Herne!* Herne the Hunter. It *was* you on the train like I thought.'

Jed put another bullet through the screen, aiming low and left, making Barrell yell out again.

'Where's that bastard Ryder? Cal! Cal!!' He fired another couple of shots at the hut, sending splinters of stone whining into the air around the working.

'He'll get his, Luke.'

'What do you want, Herne?'

'I'm paid to get the printing plates back for the money.'

'Cal's got them. Let me try and trick him out and you can take them and let me go.'

'You're a real nice guy, Luke Barrell. There's somethin' else.'

'What?'

In the silence Jed could clearly hear him spinning the chamber of his pistol and trying to reload it quietly; a muffled curse as he dropped a shell in the snow.

'Fingers gettin' cold, Luke?'

'Some. And that bullet in my leg don't help none.'

'What about the other one?'

'Took a finger of skin off my ribs, Herne. That's pretty shootin', blind up there. You got a Sharps or somethin'? Sounds like a Fed cannon.'

'It's a Sharps, Luke. Minute or so and I'm going to pepper that screen of yourn.'

'No. Give me a break.'

'I want the pendant you stole from the coffin, Luke. Where is it?'

'Cal's got that as well. It was the Mex who robbed the

girl's corpse, and Cal took the necklace off of him. She kin of yours, Herne?'

'Yeah. So he's got the plates and he's got the pendant? That right?'

'Yeah.' There was a note of hope in the man's voice. 'That's right.'

'Fine,' yelled Herne. 'Means I got only one thing to say to you.'

'What?'

'Goodbye, Luke.'

Chapter Twelve

The fourth bullet killed him.

The powerful slugs of the long rifle tore great chunks of wood from the screen, opening it up and enabling Herne to see his target clearly.

Already slowed down by the wounds to his ribs and to his leg, Barrell wasn't able to keep moving fast enough. The first and second shots missed, but they ripped away enough of the frail wall for Jed to be able to take an easy bead on the prone figure.

At the last moment Luke Barrell, his white collar a gleaming bull's eye target for the rifle, glanced round and saw that his cover had vanished. He snapped off a couple of shots from his pistol and started to make for the safety of one of the heaps of wire and wood that littered the area at the top of the Norwich Hills mine.

Neither bullet came close enough to worry Jed, and he was able to squeeze the trigger of the Sharps. Blinking through the smoke of the shot he saw Barrell flung sideways by the impact of the fifty-five calibre bullet. The Colt flying from his hand and clanging away into the debris that peeked out among the snow.

'Jesus Christ!' he screamed, the cry bouncing and echoing around the lofty walls of the Pinaleno Mountains.

Herne had aimed for a safe body hit, not wanting to risk a killing head shot, in case he missed and the wounded bandit got holed up among the rubble. As far as he could judge, the bullet had struck the phoney priest below the heart on the left side, angling down and landing up somewhere among the sack of intestines in the centre of the pelvis.

Barrell rolled about, legs kicking up the snow, hands grabbing at his body in an effort to stop the pain. Pain that paralysed him, blanking out his mind to everything else. Making him ignore the fact that he lay less than a hundred paces from Jed Herne's Sharps, helpless for the next bullet.

The fourth bullet.

Hissing softly between his teeth, Jed levered the shell into the warm breech, easing his shoulders and moving the barrel slightly against the boulders. Altering the angle to compensate for Luke Barrell's new position.

Finger on the trigger, drawing breath. And holding it.

Although the bandit was still screaming, the breath bubbling through his bloodied lips, he was moving slower, boot-heels digging furrows through the ice and grey snow, puddling it crimson with his blood. His head was on one side, the eyes screwed close shut with the agony of the gut shot, unaware of anything.

The bullet hit him just above the right ear, killing him instantly, the body relaxing, arms hanging loose and limp, fingers opening wide.

'So long, Reverend,' said Herne.

Amazingly, the thick walls of the hut had prevented Cal Ryder, the leader of the gang, from hearing the gun battle outside. Smoke still curled from the small chimney, and the door remained firmly closed.

It crossed Herne's mind that the man might be faking, but with no windows he could have no way of knowing what was going on. And it would be beyond the patience and curiosity of anyone not to at least peer out through the door to see what was happening.

Moving carefully, holding the reloaded rifle in his hand, Jed edged his way around the face of the slope until he was in a position to cover the door of the hut. There was a keyhole halfway down the right side, and a brass handle, now corroded to a dark green colour.

Easing himself down among another heap of jagged red stones, Herne got ready to deal out the last hand of cards in a game that had already covered better than a hundred miles and cost the lives of a half-dozen people.

The bullet was perfectly aimed, hitting the door handle and exploding it into whining shards of metal. He rammed in another shell, and sent it winging after the first, ripping a chunk of wood as large as a man's fist from the side of the door, startlingly white against the stained old timber.

'Luke?'

The voice was fuzzy, Cal sounding only half-awake.

A third shot actually made the door move, easing it open against the shattered latch. For a moment Herne saw the paleness of a face in the gap, then it was quickly pulled back.

'That you, Luke?'

'Luke's gone to meet his Maker, Ryder,' shouted Jed. 'Guess he'll be waiting for you.'

'Who the Hell are you? You the one called Herne the Hunter?'

'That's what they say.'

'You got Luke?'

'Sure did. Unless he's fakin' with half his head blowed clear away.'

'What do you want?'

'You.'

'Come on, Herne. You get paid for takin' back these money plates. Not for killin' me.'

'I get paid for the plates. You and the pendant you stole from the little girl's body are just for me. Get that, Ryder, just for me!'

He emphasized his words with another bullet in the door, edging it open a few inches further.

'How you aim to get me out there?'

'I don't. I aim to sit here and blow away that cover bit by bit. Then I'll walk down slow and easy and start shooting inside the hut. Big fifty-five bullet'll bounce a ways round stone walls like you got there.'

There was a silence. To help the time pass and convince Ryder of the truth of his words, Herne plugged three more shots into the door, aiming at the hinges this time. Shattering the top one.

'All right!'

'All right, what?'

'How about a deal, Herne?'

'I don't figure that you got many cards in your hand, Ryder.'

'There's hard and there's easy. You know that better'n most.'

'What's easy?'

'I throw out the plates and I come with hands up high.'

'The pendant?'

'I'll throw that out now. Here it is. Show you I mean what I say. How about it?'

'Let's see the necklace first. Followed by your guns.'

'Here it is.'

The pale light sparkled redly on the rubies in the small necklace as it flew through the half-open door and landed a few yards away in the snow.

Herne was ready for a trick, knowing that someone who led his gang like Cal Ryder did wasn't about to come out slow and easy.

So when the grey figure erupted from the door, Jed was ready for him. Sighting and firing the big rifle quick as lightning, seeing the bullet strike home.

Strike home on the *blankets*!!

While he'd been talking, Ryder had been quickly knotting three blankets together to make a rough dummy, knowing that Herne would be looking for someone making a break and might well snap off a shot before he would really see who . . . or what . . . it was.

'God damn!' cursed Jed, frantically reloading the rifle, ducking as Ryder followed closely behind the dummy. He must have known that it would take Herne a few seconds to eject the spent shell and sight and aim again. Ryder came out shooting, the bullets from his pistol ricocheting among the rocks, sending splinters of stone and ice whistling alarmingly about Jed's ears. Though there wasn't any real danger at that range of a hit, Ryder was good enough for Jed not to want to take any chances.

By the time he counted six shots fired and came up with the Sharps, Ryder was out of sight. But the snow betrayed his position. Tracks leading to the jumble of twisted equipment that surrounded the open hole of the deep shaft of the mine.

Leading to it and not leading away again the other side.

'What the Hell good has that done you, Ryder? One trap for another.'

'Maybe not.'

Herne's eyes desperately searched the debris for a clue to exactly where the bandit was hidden, unable to spot him among the pools of deep shadow.

'I said that it could be not, Herne.'

'I hear you.'

'I can see you, and you don't see me. You move from those

rocks and I can pick you off like skinning a dead chicken. Easy.'

'You try a shot and I see you, Ryder.'

'Try moving, Mister Herne the damned Hunter and you won't see the flash. They say you don't see the one that hits you.'

Herne didn't reply, trying to guess from the pitch of Cal Ryder's voice just where he was. Guessing that he must be near the middle, which meant close to the hole.

'I don't hear you so good, Herne! You want to talk about a deal now?'

'Deal's the same. I kill you now or the law kills you later. Makes no odds to me, Ryder. Figures you want to go on livin' a whiles longer, so you come out and come out slow and easy. No tricks this time.'

'Good one, wasn't it?' Cal Ryder laughed with what sounded like genuine amusement.

'Works once. Like all good tricks. It's a long cold day here, Ryder. You're not goin' to be doin' much movin' round down there.'

'Nor you up there, Herne.'

Jed wasn't able to work out just where the gunman was, or whether he was bluffing about being able to draw a fast bead on him. It was possible, and in the confusion of the escape from the hut he hadn't noticed whether the bandit had been carrying a rifle or not.

Certainly he'd snapped off shots from a pistol.

'You got the plates there, Ryder?'

'Sure. You want to see them, Herne?'

Jed didn't reply at first, wondering at the weight of the printing plates. If they were like any other plates he'd ever seen they'd be heavy. Damned heavy. With those and shooting off the handgun, it seemed doubtful that Ryder really had a rifle at all.

But you don't get old taking too many chances.

'Yeah. Show me one of them.'

'I show it, then you talk about a deal with me?'

'After I see it, then maybe we get to talk. Just maybe we do.'

'That ain't much,' said Ryder in a complaining voice, and Herne felt the elation of certainty that he didn't have a rifle. And at that range Herne was more or less safe from handgun sniping.

'All you get, boy. Show me.'

It was obvious that Ryder was having second thoughts about the wisdom of revealing his position to a hidden marksman with a Sharps buffalo gun. The chill wind was biting through Herne's clothes and nipping at the ends of his fingers. Too much of that sort of exposure and neither of them would be riding back to Tucson.

Concentrating all his energy he stared into the mess of iron and wood, trying to spot a hint of movement. There were some areas around the head of the shaft that he could see clean snow right out the other side. That narrowed it a lot.

When it came down to it, there were only a couple of pits of shadow big enough to hide a man. Without bothering to take too careful an aim Herne pumped a round into one of them, hearing the echo of the shot bouncing back to him from the sheer mountain wall across the canyon.

'Hey!'

'Close?'

'Damn it! I thought we was goin' to have us a deal! You gotta trust me!'

'Sure. Like the folks on that train trusted you not to blow the whole damned shooting-match to Hell and back again.'

'I got the plates!'

'I don't believe you.'

Another shot, this time into the other area of darkness. The shout later and less worried.

'Wait on there, Herne. Don't get so damned all-fired impatient about this!'

'You got three seconds to show me those plates and then I start shootin' again. Just three seconds, Ryder, to try and save your skin.'

'Here!'

Just to the left of where the first bullet had gone, very close to the edge of the gaping chasm, Herne saw a hand appear, holding a package wrapped in cream-coloured leather.

At a hundred yards it wasn't possible for Herne to make out which way Ryder was lying on the snow, or he'd have risked a blind shot at him, figuring to cripple him and then come in close and take him with the hand-gun.

'You see it?'

'I see it. How do I know what it is?'

'Hell! Damn it, Herne! You think I wrapped up a parcel of bread and jerky to try and fool you?'

'Open it and show me.'

The hand vanished out of sight again, and Jed Herne made his move. Trusting that the snow would cover the noise, he rolled out from cover and slid down the steep slope, his grey blanket flapping about his chest, aiming for a rusting truck off the cable railway that had once taken ore down the hill to the township.

He reached it without Ryder even suspecting that he had changed his position, and he was able to cat-foot around the side of the truck, pistol cocked in his left hand, and the Sharps braced against his right hip. Not a position that made for accurate shooting, but he was now less than thirty yards from the bandit's hiding-place.

This time he could see the man's arm, right clear to the

shoulder, with a gleaming rectangle of heavy metal clutched in the hand. Herne was even close enough to make out the engraving on the printing plate. To see the shine of the pearl buttons on Cal Ryder's fancy coat.

Tucking the Colt in his belt, Herne brought the rifle to the aim, sighting at the shoulder.

'You see it now, Herne, you stinkin' son of a bitch bastard?'

'Yeah,' whispered Jed, 'I see it, Ryder.'

The rifle kicked against his shoulder as he fired. He immediately dropped it and drew the pistol with fluid ease, diving to his right to shelter behind an ice-crusted pillar of mangled iron.

'Ooooooh!' yelped Ryder, the plate dropping from his fingers, rolling back out of sight, unable to see where the shot had come from.

'Plenty more, Ryder,' warned Herne.

When the man answered, his voice was weak and shaken. 'You stinkin' double-crosser, Herne. You promised me we'd talk after I showed you those fuckin' printin' plates!'

'We're talkin', Ryder. I said nothing about not shooting you if I had the chance.'

'Why do you hate me so much?' The tone was one of righteous indignation, like a dowager at a New York theatre when she finds someone has taken her seat.

'Not for the train. Not for the plates. Not for trying to kill me. Well, maybe some for that.'

'What then?'

'That pendant belonged to someone that I ... that I loved. I killed the rest of your scum for that, and you're about to go the same way.'

Ryder was silent for a moment, then he gave a great cry; a wordless bellow of anger and challenge. He leaped out from behind his shelter, standing poised on the very brink of the drop. Under one arm he held the plates, gripping them tight against his body. In the right hand he carried a pistol. A Colt much like Jed's.

Streaking down his body from the top of his right arm was a ribbon of scarlet, soaking wetly through the smart black coat, dappling the snow as he moved.

Herne was partly behind cover, but Ryder's move meant that he couldn't see him clearly. He was forced to come out into the open, diving to his left, firing as he fell. Coming up into a shootist's crouch, blasting off two more bullets at the bandit.

Blood gouted from three wounds.

Herne hadn't missed once. Ryder never had so much as the chance to squeeze the trigger on his own gun.

The impact of the forty-five calibre bullets rocked him off his feet, and he teetered on the edge of the deep shaft. The gun fell away, landing in the trampled ice, but he still clutched the printing plates to him like a miser hoarding his gold.

His face was a bizarre mask of blood where the last shot had caught him on the turn, drilling a hole through both cheeks. Burning a weal across the top of his tongue, splintering teeth from each side of his jaw. The other two bullets had both hit Ryder in the chest, smashing ribs and lungs, one exiting and burying itself in one of the legs of the old derrick. The other remaining inside his body.

Ryder didn't know all this.

All he knew was that the tall bastard with the old blanket blowing in the wind had just finished him. His mind began to blur and he aimed his empty right hand at the advancing figure, unable to understand why there was no explosion and no recoil.

'Give me the plates, Ryder.' The command floated in from a very long way off. Ryder shook his head. He seemed to be swaying on the edge of a great drop, and decided vaguely that this must be what dying felt like. Not aware that he was actually swaying on the brink of the deep mine-shaft, eyes blinking, body rocking backwards and forwards.

Herne thought of the three thousand dollars and called out again to the dying man. 'Give me the damned plates!'

Cal Ryder shook his head to try and clear his fading vision, aware that he felt very cold. Seeing Herne close to him, reaching out.

He even tried a grin at the last, his voice bubbling painfully up through a cauldron of frothing blood.

'Up your ass, Herne,' he said.

And slid backwards into the pit, taking the printing plates with him.

Chapter Thirteen

Jed didn't count the seconds, but it took a long time for the noises to stop. First, a wet thud as the corpse bounced off a ledge. Then another, deeper and quieter. Followed by the crash of stones and debris as they dragged on down after the falling body. Then smaller pebbles that clattered and tinkled on long after the rest of the noise had stopped.

Only when it was quite silent did he take the final steps forward and peer down into the blackness. Not that he expected to see anything, but he felt he had to do something.

A little fine dust, like smoke, came drifting sullenly up from the damp chasm, until the wind picked it apart and scattered it across the Pinalenos Mountains.

Herne holstered his pistol and began picking his way through the treacherous heap of distorted metal, until he was right on the edge of the Norwich Hills shaft. Far, far below there was the faint sound of something shifting in the blackness. Something settling.

He bent and picked up a lump of stone. Flicking the powdery snow from it. Lobbing it into the hole. Waiting until he heard the dull thunk as it hit the bottom. It was so far down that there wasn't any point in trying to climb down, even if he'd had the means to get there and back on his own.

'Either bring the plates back or see they're safely destroyed' had been his mission. They couldn't be much safer than they were down the shaft, thought Herne. But to make even more sure he levered several of the larger chunks of débris down the pit. Iron and rotting wood in a cascade that stirred the echoes for nearly a full minute.

'Anyone gets them out, then by God but they're damned welcome to them,' he muttered, turning away.

On the walk back down the steep slope into the tottering remnants of the township, Herne picked up the rifle and the pendant. Putting the tiny necklace safely away in an inside pocket, having made sure that none of the jewels had been disturbed; that it was still perfect.

It was all right. The rubies still glistened in their heart-shaped setting, reflecting the pale light of the winter's day like watered-down blood.

The ride back to Tucson was easy. He saw nobody. Nobody except for the shadowy figures that haunted the further edges of the hills, occasionally silhouetted against the dull sky. Man Runs On Air was making sure that Herne left his territory safely.

The snow that had threatened never came, and the sun was shining brightly as he cantered down the main street of Tucson two days later. The eating-house was closed up, with boards across the smashed front door. His room had been kept for him, and after a steaming hot bath he went straight to bed, leaving instructions that he wasn't to be interrupted by anybody. And not by Mister Jollye especially.

When he woke it was well into the afternoon. The sky was still blue and clear with visibility as far as the eye could see in every direction. It was a good day to be alive.

He considered calling in on the sheriff to put in a claim for the bounty on Barrell and Ryder, but decided against it. He hadn't fancied dragging Luke's corpse all the way back to town, and bounties were rarely paid on missing bodies.

Not even their horses had been worth keeping. Spavined

nags with ribs sticking through their faded coats. Herne had released them from the Norwich Hills mine and let them go free, figuring that the Apaches would find some kind of use for them.

As he came down the stairs of the rooming-house, freshly shaved, with his cleaned Colt swinging on his hip, the Government agent leaped to his feet from the lobby where he'd been waiting.

'Herne! They wouldn't let me up to see you!'

'Right. Told them I'd take them off at the knees if they let anyone up.'

'Well?'

'Fine.'

Jollye's face lit up with relief and pleasure. 'You killed them all?'

'That's right. I shot them all dead. You want a description of where each bullet went?'

'No. Of course not. But they *are* all dead?'

'And cold.'

The agent stood off a couple of steps and looked up at him. 'Where are the plates? In your room? Dangerous to leave them there, Mister Herne. Maybe we should go up and get them?'

'The girl got the money?'

'What?'

'The money. Ellie-May Mitchell. For buryin' her Grandpa. She get it?'

'Yes. Of course. I am a man of my word, Mister Herne. I say precisely what I mean and I stand by that. Now, the printing plates.'

'I don't have them.'

If he'd unbuttoned his trousers and relieved himself over the agent's boots he couldn't have got a more dramatic result. All the blood drained from the little man's face and he swayed. For a moment Herne thought he was going to faint but with a great effort he recovered.

'Wh . . .' He cleared his throat and tried once more. 'What do you mean?'

'I mean, I don't have them.'

'Who does?'

'Nobody.'

'Don't try jokes on with me, Herne. It is a matter of the greatest gravity.'

'Well, if anyone has them then Cal Ryder does.'

'You said that he was . . .'

'Dead. He is. Very. He's at the bottom of a mine shaft high in the Pinalenos.'

'But . . .'

'With a few tons of old timber and rusty iron holding him down. And four bullets for company. He's got the plates. He took them with him when he fell.'

He could almost feel the relief from Jollye. In a nervous gesture the agent turned to a large gilt mirror at his elbow, decorated at the edges with fat cherubs, and adjusted his necktie, drawing deep breaths as he recovered his composure. When he faced Herne again there was a foxy smile on his lips. A smile that stopped a long way short of his eyes.

'So there is no chance of them ever being reached?'

'Absolutely none at all.'

'They are safe there?'

'Sure.'

'I have your word on that?'

'Sure. I give you my word that nobody will ever be able to get those plates. Only you and me know where they are, and I'm not going back.'

Jollye nodded. 'Excellent. I have been making enquiries about you, Mister Herne. All say that you are a man of total violence. And total honesty. I believe you.'

'Good. I'll be having the three thousand dollars. I got things to do this afternoon, and then I want to be moving on.'

'Ah.'

'What the Hell does that mean?'

'It means that I merely wish to see your proof that the plates have been effectively destroyed.'

'I told you, and you said you believed me.'

'Yes. If I recall my words, and I am a careful man with words, I said that I would pay you two thousand dollars to go and three thousand dollars for the return of the plates. Or irrefutable evidence that you have destroyed them.'

Herne stood very still, feeling his fingers itching for the butt of the Colt. He knew men of Jollye's type. Men who would send others to do the dirty work and then complain that not all of the 'i's had been dotted and some of the 't's weren't crossed.

'I am sorry. I personally believe you. But in the work of Government one has to be careful what one does. That is the first rule of business and it is as clear as the nose on my face. I am grateful to you for your efforts, Mister Herne and I bid you good-day.'

'Wait on.'

'What?'

Jed Herne had learned long ago that there were times when it was as well to cut your losses and move on. Maybe if he wrangled long enough he might get some of that three thousand dollars back. Maybe. But he wanted satisfaction, and there was a better, quicker way.

'Plain as the nose on your face, Mister Jollye?' he said.

'Yes.'

'Look at your nose in that mirror, Mister Jollye,' he went on. 'Look good. And say good-day to it.'

'Why?'

'I'm about to make it a mite plainer.'

Herne seized the back of the agent's head in both hands, locking his fingers tightly into the greasy hair. And rammed Jollye's face as hard as he was able into the gilt-framed mirror. The glass split into a hundred razor-edged fragments, and Jollye's nose cracked. Grunting with the effort, Jed tugged back and then ground the man's face into the remains of the glass, knocking out most of his front teeth, snapping them off at the roots. Spreading the broken nose halfway across his cheeks, and cutting his face to ribbons on the splintered shards of the mirror.

Jollye tried to scream once, but the impact of the second blow knocked him out. He hung limply in Herne's hands, until the big shootist dropped him to the carpet of the lobby, stepping back to avoid getting the streams of blood on his boots.

The owner of the rooming-house watched the scene in frozen horror, recoiling when Jed turned to him.

'You see what happened?'

'No, Sir. Yes, Sir. I mean . . .'

'Saw him trip and bang into that mirror?'

The hand dropped to the Colt, and the man whitened. 'I guess I did.'

Jollye was still being sewed up at the doctor's when Herne rode Jubal out of Tucson with the remnants of the money in his saddle-bag. The sheriff had stared hard at him, and Jed had stared right back.

The sun was sinking far down in the west when he finally reached the three mounds near the stream. He had thought about replacing the pendant in the coffin, but had pulled back from the idea, wanting to try and keep a memory of how Becky had been and not what she would now have become.

So he scraped a hole in the small grave, a foot or so deep, and placed the pendant in it, patting the earth back down over it. Standing up and sighing with the effort.

Looking down at all that was now left of his past life. Trying to think of something to say. The words freezing in his throat.

'So long, Becky. Mrs. Yates. So long, Louise. I'll never forget what . . .'

But there was still a long way to go and time was running short.

He swung easily up into the saddle and heeled the stallion forwards. Away towards the setting sun.

At the top of the nearest ridge he paused, seeing the trail winding away below him. If he looked back he would be able to see the shadows of the three graves.

Keeping his face to the golden sky in the west, Jed Herne rode on.

Alone.

THE END